ECCLESALL

CW00740238

Sheffield
City Council

Renew this item at:
http://library.sheffield.gov.uk
or contact your local library

LIBRARIES, ARCHIVES & INFORMATION

For Fearne and Erin; our very own beacon of hope.

A. J. Brown

THE PANACEUM

Part 1: Providence

AUSTIN MACAULEY PUBLISHERS™

LONDON • CAMBRIDGE • NEW YORK • SHARJAH

A CIP catalogue record for this title is available from the British Library.

ISBN 9781398497054 (Paperback)
ISBN 9781398497061 (ePub e-book)

First Published 2023
Austin Macauley Publishers Ltd®
1 Canada Square
Canary Wharf
London
E14 5AA

Seven years, two babies, and one global pandemic in the making, it is wonderful to see our book come to print. There are so many people to thank.

We are immensely lucky in that the unwavering support of our families is a given, but we would like to take this opportunity to say that it is never taken for granted.

Then, to Emma and Jo, who believed in our story from the outset and whose feedback was pivotal in shaping the work throughout.

Thank you, Corinne, for your eagle eyes and enthusiasm.

And finally, thank you to everyone at Austin Macauley, without whom none of this would have been possible.

panacea

noun

pan·a·cea | \ ˌpa-nə-ˈsē-ə \

a solution or remedy for all difficulties or diseases.

Chapter One

Heaven exists. Everyone knows that.

We've all seen the videos: smiles, sunshine, promises.

I know why we go there; I know it makes sense...

But that won't make saying goodbye to my grandmother tonight any easier.

I've spent the morning helping put together a feast of all my grandmother's favourites. My mother has given the orders as usual, and today I've gladly obeyed, thankful for the distraction. At every mention of my grandmother, my mother has just said, "'It's for the best'. 'It's what we chose', or 'One day you'll understand'." Each empty remark has made me angrier than the last, and by the time we finally stop for lunch, I'm ready to explode.

"How can you be so *okay* with this!" I spit.

"Look, we'll have this conversation when you're older."

"I'm fifteen!"

"Exactly! You're still a child."

For a second, I swear I see fire in my mother's eyes: then it's gone again, buried beneath her default calm.

"One day, you'll understand."

She rises, as if to signal the debate is over.

It is *not* over.

"Won't you miss her?" I demand, stopping her in her tracks.

"She's my mother."

Her eyes must be burning now, but she'd never give me the satisfaction of seeing them. I stare at her, willing her to turn, to shout, to cry, to do something – anything – to make me feel like I'm not the only person who actually cares. But she doesn't flinch.

"That's the price we pay for sixty years of clean health."

"And what about Dad? Where are his sixty years of clean health?"

She walks away.

I am the only kid in my class from a one-parent family, and one of only two in my school. Being Panacean should entitle you to sixty years of illness-free life, but accidents can happen. The vaccine can't account for everything: acts of nature, fate, human error. Saying that, accidents *are* rare. Slate Mason's dad was in engineering and was crushed when part of a new Citi-Bloc collapsed during construction. That was one of the biggest accidents in The Panaceum's history – it was in the news all week; it was a big deal.

My mother never mentions the death of my father. In fact, no one does, not even the obnoxious, plasticated girls at school who would love nothing more than fresh ammunition to hurl at me on a daily basis. Even they have their limits. The only person who ever mentions him at all is my grandmother, and even then, she barely scratches the surface.

And now *she's* leaving me too.

I look at all the food, the decorations, the table laid out ready for a celebration – but what is there to celebrate? After tonight, I'll never see the one person who understands me most ever again.

Never.

Tonight, is my grandmother's ascension.

Chapter Two

By 7 pm, a steady stream of guests are arriving: all shapes, all sizes, none of whom I recognise, but I guess they must be old work colleagues, friends and neighbours of my grandmother. Before long, there's hardly room to move in our hub and we're forced to open the doors to the biospace so people can spill out onto the lawn. I didn't realise my grandmother was so popular.

"Cressida, you look beautiful!"

She strokes my hair as she approaches. My grandmother is the only person who still calls me by our shared name, Cressida. Everyone else calls me Cress – just like everyone calls *her* Ida.

Cress.

Ida.

Two parts of the same person. I'll miss that.

"Thanks, you look lovely too," I reply.

And she really does. Her flowing, silver hair shines in stark contrast to the short, tight crops of the other women her age and her dress lolls carelessly and seems to dance around her feet as she weaves her way through the guests towards the centre of the room.

"Cressida!" she chirps from afar. "Come here! There's someone I'd like you to meet."

I've been so distracted by her dress that I haven't noticed that she's stopped to greet one of the most unmistakable faces here in Citi-Bloc 7. I've seen the man several times before, but never dared to look at him directly for more than a few seconds.

"Cressida, this is Ezra Shah. Ezra owns 'Laser Ink' down in The Rec."

As if I didn't already know...

The Rec, or Recreational Tri-sector, filled with bustling precincts and arcades, is open to under 18s between the hours of 3pm and 7pm – after dark, it's strictly adults only. After school, some of my class often head over to Laser Ink to check out the latest tattoo designs. I hear them talk excitedly about getting 'marked' as soon as they're old enough.

There's no point in me getting into discussions about designs or colours, even if I wanted to. My mother always says, "How can getting marked make someone an individual if everybody's doing it?"

She clearly doesn't understand.

"Pleased to meet you," says Ezra, interrupting my thoughts, "your grandmother has told me so much about you."

I freeze.

How does my grandmother know Ezra? And why on Earth would she talk to him about *me*?

His voice is deep, smooth and strangely comforting. Standing so close to Ezra, it is hard not to be overwhelmed as my eyes scan the most famous marks in all of The Panaceum.

15

Every inch of his skin is intricately patterned: symbols, drawings, words – some in languages I don't even recognise – making him look both ancient and ultra-modern all at once. His face alone is home to what looks like hundreds of detailed marks, in endless colours, all shaded in a way that makes his skull appear to be slowly emerging through his skin. Then, the skull opens to reveal a dazzling set of teeth. He is smiling. At me. And I'm staring.

I quickly turn to my grandmother, who begins to laugh heartily. Ezra joins her but I don't dare to look, for fear I'll die at the embarrassment of having been caught gawping at him like some small, dumbstruck kid. Just as I'm at the point where I feel like turning and running away as far as I can, missing my grandmother's ascension altogether, my mother's voice rings out over the crowd.

"We have a visitor!"

…It's time to get started.

*

A uniformed PCO stands beside my mother, who has taken up a prominent position in the room. All eyes are trained upon The Panacean Council Operative, who places a sleek, black pebble upon the table.

"Cressida Connors?"

My grandmother steps forward.

"The Council thanks you for your services to The Panaceum. May your journey be safe. May your years be plentiful. Heaven awaits you."

The PCO gestures for my grandmother to take a seat, but she needs little guidance – all ascensions basically follow the same format.

The reality of it all is sinking in now. Tears begin to sting behind my eyes. I hear applause and cheers from all corners of the room, led by my mother who beams ridiculously as though my grandmother is up for some sort of award.

I stare blankly, detaching myself from the crowd, until my grandmother's eyes fix me with a gaze so intense that I dare not break it. I could be looking into a mirror – her eyes are filled with the same fear and apprehension I can feel building inside of me. The crowd cheer on, unaware. Seconds pass before my mother breaks the moment, squeezing my grandmother's shoulder and flicking her eyes to the crowd as if to remind her that there are onlookers present. My grandmother conjures a smile and stretches out a raised index finger, theatrically. She places it upon the pebble before her.

Immediately, a green light activates, scanning her fingertip, confirming her identity. An array of beams shoots from the device, filling the air with a three-dimensional holo-cast of the Panacean emblem.

"Intellihub L-7. Confirm."

My mother's command sends the room into darkness, leaving only an eerie hue upon the faces of the crowd. We wait in expectant silence. It is broken by the familiar sound of the Panacean fanfare signalling the start of the council's official ascension message.

With heavy hearts we fled the old territory, and the scourge of disease brought about by our own short-sightedness and neglect.

The holo-cast projects images of life before The Panaceum: buildings spewing thick, black smoke; toxic sludge leaking into the water we once drank, hospitals crammed with bodies, reddened by sores, infected by what became known as *The New Plague*. I have seen these images before in history class, but I can't imagine a world where they actually existed. It occurs to me that to my grandmother, who was one of the very first Panaceans, they may not appear so alien.

We promised those who followed us a clean start, clean energy, and clean health. Together, we achieved what many said would be impossible. Today, The Panaceum stands as shining beacon of hope. You, Cressida Connors, have served to further our cause – now let The Panaceum reward your endeavours. Heaven awaits you.

The air fills with images of silver-haired men and women, flashing gleaming, white teeth as they smile together against sunlit backdrops. Their smiles prompt long cracks of skin to explode from the corners of their eyes, creating deep furrows in their brows and cheeks – 'wrinkles'. Their skin seems looser somehow, as if it's falling slightly from their bones. Now, they stroll along golden sands with little sign of intention, or purpose; simply content in each other's company – white teeth still gleaming.

We are then taken back to The Panaceum, where fresh-faced apprentices are shown taking their first steps into construction, public services and medicine. Student doctors appear, learning to inject babies with the Panacea vaccine, who scream even though they're being blessed with sixty years of protection against all known diseases from the life we left behind. The message continues.

In your wake, a new generation will flourish, secure in jobs and homes passed down by those who have ascended before them. In turn, they too will ascend, paving the way for future Panaceans in the centuries to follow. With that in mind, take tonight to celebrate, embrace those you love, and rest assured that they will live in good health and prosperity. May your journey be safe. May your years be plentiful. Heaven awaits you.

I hear cheers and a ripple of applause as I've come to expect at ascensions. I look to my grandmother, but rather than joining in, she stares on, unmoved. No one else appears to notice as her eyes glaze. My mother raises a glass.

"My hero, my confidante, and the bravest woman I know: my mother, Cressida Connors."

Hero? Confidante? Wow, my mother really is putting on a show.

Regardless, the crowd lap it up.
"Heaven awaits you!" they cry out in chorus.
My grandmother barely registers a smile.
If anything, she looks almost…afraid.
I've been to many ascensions.
I have never seen a reaction like it.

Chapter Three

We enter the lift in silence.
My grandmother. My mother. And me.
Three generations of Connors.
Only two will return.

It's taken us the best part of an hour to say goodbye to all of our guests. Now we are finally alone, surrounded by the cold, chrome walls of the lift. The silence in here feels strange after all the noise of the party. I want to say something, but no words come. Even my mother has nothing to say now that her 'hostess' performance has ended.

At least that's something to be thankful about.

Before us lies a vast control panel, containing a map of Citi-Bloc 7. From here, we could travel to any of the 156 levels, and to several points upon that level, horizontally or vertically. There are hundreds, perhaps thousands of destinations, each indicated by a tiny, white light, but tonight we are only interested in one. Without ceremony, my grandmother places her index finger on a separate panel labelled simply with a glowing letter 'A'.

In a lifetime, you only get to perform this action once.

Immediately, her finger is scanned, confirming her identity and the lift launches into action. I feel my stomach lurch as we pick up speed, hurtling skyward towards the Ascension Deck. We move quickly, but it will still take over a minute to travel the 156 floors we need to cover. I have never been to the roof before. Excitement swells within my stomach, but I push any sign of it away from my face.

The roof, or 'Ascension Deck' is reserved for passengers boarding the SkyRail. Two close friends or relatives are allowed to accompany boarders as far as the depot – tonight would be my first opportunity. I have heard there's no view of the city quite like it from anywhere else in The Panaceum, but as the doors to the lift slide open, I wonder if I'll catch a glimpse of the one thing that I *really* want to see…

I step outside, and immediately my throat is cut by an icy blast. A real wind. Below, the streets are so sheltered by towering Citi-Blocs and skyscrapers that barely a breeze registers, but here I welcome the blustering gales that pull the air from my lungs. The cold bites at my skin too – I should have worn warmer clothes.

My mother stands talking to a security officer – probably confirming who we all are. Beyond my mother, I can see deep into the heart of the city. People are right, I've never seen The Panaceum like this. From this height, the Residential and Enterprise Tri-sectors seem dark due to their energy restrictions at this hour, but in the distance The Rec glows – pulsing red and orange lights forcing back the night sky. Names of nightclubs – *Flesh, The Midnight Lounge, Eden* – project through the fiery hue, fighting for advertising space on the clouds above. If I close my eyes, I can almost hear their heavy bass sounds summoning adults who want to escape their everyday lives.

Empty pleasures – my mother would call them.

I am both scared and thrilled at the thought of such a place.

Impressive as it looked, I hadn't come to the roof to see parts of The Panaceum I could see every day from our biospace at home. I turn around and adjusting my eyes, I look out into the distance past the stretch of water that surrounds us and the solar farms which stand on the far shore.

Seconds go by where I can see nothing at all, only darkness which seems to stretch out into forever. Then, as if from nowhere, dots of light begin to come into focus and I finally get first-hand proof of something which, until recently, I barely even knew existed.

Life *beyond* The Panaceum.

Yet here it is, right in front of me, twinkling in the distance. Are they houses? Schools? Entire Citi-Blocs?

Growing up, I knew nothing of what lay beyond the vast waters that surround us. Everyone my age is taught that anything beyond The Panaceum belongs to the past – a wasteland, beyond repair, abandoned. The Panacea vaccine had been our saviour, and those who shunned it were left to fend for themselves against The New Plague.

Forgotten.

Then, a couple of years ago, something changed. Suddenly, videos began to surface, and in school we'd be warned about the potential threat of scavengers, rebels – those infected by The New Plague, and driven by the jealousy of not becoming Panaceans when they had the chance.

Nomarks.

I wanted to know more, but Miss Summerhythe, my class teacher, refused to talk about it. There was only one person I knew that would give me a straight answer. Even so, my grandmother only allowed me to ask one question.

"Where do they live?" I asked, after some thought.

Instead of answering, she rummaged through a box beneath her bed, and pulled out a folded and worn piece of paper. It was a map, clearly, but not one I'd seen before. At the top of the paper were the words *The United Kingdom*. I scanned the tiny print for any words that I recognised. The boldest words – London, Manchester, Edinburgh – held no significance, but eventually I came across something that jumped out at me.

Oxford.

Now, standing on the Ascension Deck of our Citi-Bloc, looking out over the water known as The Oxford Strait, it was hard to believe that this land was ever above sea level. And, if this was what had become of Oxford, then what had become of all the other towns and cities outlined on my grandmother's map? What's more, why would Miss Summerhythe refuse to tell me anything?

"Cress, get back from there!"

Without realising, I'd wandered towards the edge of the roof, drawn by the lights in the distance. I turn to see my mother, charging towards me.

"This isn't the place to be messing around," she barks, "It's time to say goodbye."

I follow my mother back to where my grandmother is stood, readying her bags as the SkyRail glides almost silently into the depot. It is made up of individual pods, suspended from a track that emerges from the heart of the city, and out into the night sky as far as the eye can see.

A vacant pod pulls up not too far from where we're standing, and for the third and final time tonight, my grandmother's finger is scanned.

"Welcome, Cressida Conners. May your journey be safe. May your years be plentiful. Heaven awaits you."

The automated voice comes from a speaker inside the pod. It really is time to say goodbye. My mother puts a hand on my shoulder which, for her, is unusually affectionate. Still, it does little to stop the choking feeling which is building in my throat. My grandmother's smile beams as she hugs my mother, long and tight, whispering messages, broken by small sobs, into her ear. Finally, they part.

"We're almost there, Althea."

My mother exhales and returns a resolute nod.

Now, it's my turn. I crumble in my grandmother's arms, drinking up the smell of her perfume, the softness of her skin, and the warmth of her cheek pressed against my own that I will never feel again.

"Always remember," she whispers, "your mother loves you…more than you can possibly know. One day, this will all make sense to you my precious, precious, child. And, of course, I love you too."

The final words are swallowed in a surge of emotion which seems to force her to board the SkyRail as quickly as she can, for fear that if she didn't do it right then, she may not do it at all.

Tears stream from her eyes as the door slides closed. A PCO nearby gives commands into a radio, and seconds later the SkyRail whirrs into motion – Heaven-bound – taking my grandmother, and all those whose contract with The Panaceum has come to an end today, out into the night.

*

Remembering watching the string of lights disappear into the distance, I had no idea that sitting by my bed was a note, written in my grandmother's hand, that would turn everything I thought I knew about The Panaceum completely on its head, forever.

Chapter Four

Five. Little. Words.

I've thought of nothing else all week long. How can five words alter everything you thought you'd known for fifteen years of your life?

It's now Sunday. A week has passed since I said goodbye to my grandmother. Seven days since I got my first glimpse of a world beyond The Panaceum. Seven days since I discovered the note that my grandmother had left me...

School has been a blur, nights are spent in silence with my mother, who seems to have been hit harder than I expected by the ascension. I am alone in my room having told her I need to study before school tomorrow. I'm not studying. I sit, holding the note. I don't need to read it; I know it by heart. Still, I run over it in my mind, trying to unlock some sort of code, or secret meaning behind the words. Can it really be as simple as it sounds?

My eyes are drawn to the top of my left arm. It holds the only mark my mother will ever allow me to have, the one all Panaceans are given on the day that they are born: the mark of the Panacea vaccine. My fingers trace the outline of the shape which is made up of two symbols from the old world:

one representing health, and the other symbolising everything that could put that health in danger.

The vaccine is actually made up of over 60 individual injections. The Panaceum emblem offers some cover for the scar tissue that can be left behind once the skin is healed. Because of this, everyone's mark is slightly different.

I remember, last year, I was in Art class and Miss Summerhythe asked us to partner up with someone and take turns to draw each other's Panacea marks. She asked us to think about the colours, textures and contours that made our marks unique. I worked with Kenzi Verhoff. I closed my eyes and nervously ran my hand over her skin. Sure enough, I could feel small indentations and a raised section near the top of her mark where the scar tissue had over-healed. I tried my best to show this in my drawing, but I'm no artist.

Then, when it came to drawing my vaccination scar, Kenzi's hand shot into the air.

"Miss, miss!" she screamed across the classroom, "Feel this!"

I feared the worst – there was something horrendously wrong with my scar and the girls who already sniggered behind my back would have something else to add to their arsenal.

In fact, it was exactly the opposite.

"Well, well, well," Miss Summerhythe said through a beaming smile, "this is very special."

She ran her fingers over my upper arm, and I followed her lead. I'd never really taken much notice in the past, but now I realised my skin was even and smooth compared to Kenzi's.

"Cress here has a 'perfect heal' everyone! Her Panacea mark has healed almost perfectly, with no major indentations or noticeable lumps and bumps. It's not unheard of for this to happen, but it is quite unusual. Would you mind if some of the others have a feel, Cress?"

I reluctantly agreed, but then immediately regretted it as the entire class queued up to stroke my arm as I sat blushing and squirming in my seat. Skyla Pearce tried her best to look unimpressed as she dragged her fingertips towards my elbow.

"Great. Maybe you could be an arm model..." She yawned, eyes rolling skywards as she walked away.

It didn't matter though – to most of the class, I'd suddenly become just a little bit more interesting. It was a good day. I spoke to more people the rest of that week than I had during my entire time at the school.

By the following week, it had all been forgotten.

Still, 'perfect heal' or not, it didn't bring me any closer to understanding the note that my grandmother had left for me.

I look out into the night, wondering where she might be.

Of course, I already know the answer.

Heaven.

But if Heaven exists and The Panacea works, then surely the note *can't* make any sense?

Frustrated, I fold it away and put it back under my pillow. I'll not sleep again tonight. Instead, those five little words will churn around in my brain, still struggling to find sense.

WHEN ILLNESS COMES, FIND EZRA.

Chapter Five

Time has passed and sleeping has become easier. Slowly, thoughts of the note have become mixed up with other things: school, friends and my mother – who still isn't herself since my grandmother left six weeks ago. I look at the note every night, but now as more of a comforting reminder. I try to imagine her in Heaven, walking along those perfect beaches, laughing with new friends she's made, or perhaps old friends who had gone to Heaven before her. Who knows? Either way, I hope she is happy.

And knowing my grandmother, she'd left the note for a very good reason. I don't know that reason, but I'm sure it will become clear exactly when my grandmother intends it to. So for now, I've decided to get on with things. But the note and the ascension have made me see The Panaceum through slightly different eyes. Recently, I've noticed more signs of a potential threat from outsiders. Maybe they've been here all along and I haven't realised, but now, everywhere I turn, there seems to be some warning of the dangers posed by intruders.

I first noticed it walking home from school one day. I'd had a run-in with Skyla Pearce again in class – the last thing I wanted to do was share a bus home with her and her cronies. I decided to walk. Walking is not advised by our school: it's quite a distance between the Enterprise and Residential Tri-sectors, and it means passing through the areas surrounding Citi-Blocs 1 and 2. They were the first Citi-Blocs to be built when The Panaceum was founded. As time's gone by, and bigger, more advanced Citi-Blocs have shot up around them, the older ones have become dated, and undesirable. The cheaper accommodation attracts lower paid workers, loners, and those who spend any money they get their hands on at The Rec. Still, I thought, how bad can it be?

As I approached Citi-Bloc 1, I found myself regretting not taking the bus. Citi-Bloc 7, where I live, is clean and bright, with maintained grounds. This was completely different. It was eerily quiet, I guess most of the people who live here work at The Rec through the night, and sleep during the day. Everything that would usually be gleaming chrome or polished glass seemed to be covered with a layer of grime. Every surface on ground level was tagged with graffiti. Names, slogans and pictures covered the walls, and they were littered with posters of all shapes and sizes. Most were advertising nightclubs and casinos in The Rec, but one stood out among the rest. It read:

SAY 'NO' TO NOMARKS. SYMPATHISERS WILL BE PROSECUTED.

'Nomark' is a slang name given to people from outside of The Panaceum who've not been vaccinated, but I'd never seen it used on official council material. This, however, held the seal of The Panacean Council, and seemed to be suggesting that Nomarks had potentially entered our community already.

I froze. Could this possibly be true? I suddenly became aware that although the streets were empty, anybody could be peering out from the hundreds of windows towering above me. Watching me. Weighing me up. Perhaps I was being paranoid, but I started walking briskly without looking up and headed home as quickly as I could.

Shaken, but unharmed, I thought little more of the poster until, two weeks later, more posters commissioned by The Panacean Council began to appear – this time on billboards, in e-zines, and even on the side of taxi cabs.

ANTI-VAXXERS: ANTI-PANACEUM. ANTI-SAFETY. ANTI-PROGRESS.

Again, the poster held the official seal of the council, but they were no longer restricted to one area. They were in every Citi-Bloc, and every Tri-Sector of The Panaceum. The wording had changed – 'Nomarks' had become 'Anti-vaxxers' – but the message was very much the same: a threat existed, and it was now close enough to worry about.

I want to speak to my mother about it all, but she's been so distant lately that I doubt she's even noticed anything different. Besides, she's been leaving for work so early, and locking herself away to do more work once she's home, that I've barely seen her. Now though, I am waiting at the breakfast table for her to emerge from her room. It's Friday – her day off, though she's usually an early riser. I've made coffee, which is starting to get cold.

Impatient, I pick up the coffee and head to her room, knocking on the door. I hear a mumble, which I take as permission to enter, and step inside. I expect to find her reading or catching up on the week's news, but it's dark – her shades still drawn – and she lies in bed barely stirring from her sleep. She's obviously working far too hard – I'll mention that in our little conversation too.

"I brought you some coffee," I whisper, conscious that she still seems groggy.

"You...shouldn't..." she replies, then contorts her face through the gloom in a way that I think is meant to be a smile.

"They're working you too hard. It's nearly 8 o'clock. I thought we could have breakfast together before school."

"I...outside...go outside..." my mother groans.

"But I brought you some – "

"Get out!" she screams. "Get out!"

I stand, gobsmacked.

I would shout back at her.

I want to.

But then, she begins coughing.

Chapter Six

"What was that?" I stammer, fearing the answer.

None comes.

"What the hell was that?"

Nothing.

I run to the window and hammer the button to release the shutters. Slowly, light fills the room, unveiling a scene unlike anything I've ever known.

Beside my mother, there are piles of handkerchiefs on a table, along with vitamins and a whole host of implements I don't recognise. My mother's hair is wet and sticks to her brow. Her eyes seem dark, her nose red and her chest convulses as she gulps the air.

"Mum?"

I don't want an explanation now: I'll settle for any kind of response.

I rush towards her, placing a trembling hand upon her forearm. Her skin burns against my palm and glows so crimson that you can barely see the outline of her Panacea mark. Her eyes are closed, and as I shake her, there is no sign of life in her limbs. She obviously used the last of her energy yelling at me to leave.

I can't leave.

My head is swimming, but I need to focus.

What would my mother do?

Frantic, I run to the bathroom and set the shower to cold; back to the bedroom, dragging my mother to the edge of the bed. The sheets cling to her damp body, and I peel them away from her back. I know there will be no easy way to do this, so I take a deep breath, bending at the knees, and prepare to take her full weight. After some panicked adjustments, I manage it, but my grip slips on her sweat-sleeked skin and I only just manage to get through the bathroom door before my mother and I fall, fully clothed, under the icy torrents of water. I yelp in shock. I'm really not sure whether I am doing the right thing, but I am doing the best I know how.

Soaked, I prop my mother against the corner of the shower cubicle and make my way into the lounge.

"Intellihub: Activate. Call…"

A ping sounds, which lets me know that our Hub's intelligence system is awaiting further instruction. Do I call a doctor? Nurse? There are emergency services I can contact, but is this even an emergency? I have no idea. I think back to my mother's room – the handkerchiefs, the vitamins. This is not a surprise to my mother: she has been keeping it from me. Why had she not contacted a doctor herself?

"Call incoming."

What?

"Call incoming," repeated the computerised voice of Intellihub.

"Intellihub: Reject," I command, more out of surprise than anything else. Only a few seconds pass before the air is once again broken by the computerised voice.

"Call incoming."

This time, I leave the call to go through to our voicemail service. I hear my mother's recorded voice apologising for not being able to answer and asking the caller to leave a message.

"Mrs Conners. Systems show unexplained absence from work yesterday. Please report to Duty Manager: Extension 171 pending further investigation into the matter. Thank you."

Absent?

Absence of any kind is rare. How on earth was my mother going to explain this? That was a problem for another time: right now, she was in no fit state to explain anything. Then, another thought hits me: school will realise my own absence within a few minutes if I don't show. That would spell even more trouble.

I need to go.

Wheeling around, I rush back into the bathroom, where my mother sits, now shivering, where I'd left her. I turn off the water, and lift her chin, which is slumped upon her chest. Her eyes focus on me for the first time since I found her.

"I need to get you back to bed," I say, trying overly hard to sound calm. "You need to help me. Okay?"

My mother seems to process the words, then brings her knees up to her chest. From there, we rise and stumble our way back to the bedroom. I just make it to the bed before my mother's weight becomes too much and we both collapse. I strip off her wet clothes and sling them into a corner of the room. I have never seen my mother naked before; in fact, she would be mortified if she knew. Now is not the time to care. I grab her bath robe and tuck it around her body, hoping that it will soak up some of the moisture. Her skin is so hot, that it dries almost instantly, and I replace the bath robe with a light sheet in an attempt to keep her cool.

Looking at the time, I have little choice but to quickly change, collect my things and hope that my mother will be stable until I get home.

"Mum? Mum, listen to me," I shout, "I need to go to school, or they are going to ask questions. I'll be back as soon as I can. Please, just…"

It's pointless. She clearly isn't registering the words. I head to the door and look back one final time at my mother, whose frail body still shivers beneath the bedsheet. Then, the shivering seems to become more pronounced. She begins twitching erratically and within a few seconds, the shivering has turned into violent shaking. She writhes uncontrollably, contorting her whole body into unnatural shapes, and finally lets out long groans of anguish.

I can't bear it.

Without thinking, I pounce on top of her and hold on for dear life. I try my best to stop her flailing limbs, but she is far too strong, and I take a blow to the side of the face. After a few hazy seconds, my senses return and I clamp her limbs in a tight bear-hug. Still, she fights me with everything she has. Her tongue hangs loosely from her open mouth, and her eyes roll around untethered.

I realise I'm crying.

I barely recognise this woman.

Twisted.

Drooling.

This is not my mother.

I hold on tighter, begging her to stop, but my efforts only seem to make her fight even harder.

Then, in an instant, she's still.

I wait to make sure that it's not a temporary calm, then carefully unwrap my body from hers. Looking at her now, there's little sign of the fight that just took place. She almost looks peaceful.

One thing's for certain: there is no way I'm leaving her in this state – trouble or no trouble. And anyway, I can't help thinking that whatever is happening here is something far bigger than any decision about whether or not I go to school today…

Chapter Seven

I've spent the past hour watching the gentle rise and fall of my mother's chest. She's calmer now, but she still hasn't opened her eyes.

Her skin burns.

My stomach groans, cutting through the silence and I realise that I haven't eaten all morning. I figure it must be nearly lunchtime, and then wonder how long it had been since my mother had last eaten. Making my way to the kitchen, I pin my hopes on finding something easy to feed to my mother. It feels odd to be at home during the middle of the day. It's quiet – really quiet. I've never missed school before. In fact, I can't remember anyone from my class missing a day of school.

I root through the cupboards and eventually lay my hands on a packet of vegetable soup, which I rip open, tip into a bowl and cover in boiling water. This is about as far as my skills in the kitchen will stretch. After a quick stir, I give it a taste. I can't pick out any 'vegetables'. And it's definitely more of a cloudy water than a soup…but it will do.

Eager to get back to my mother, I pick up the bowl, only to be stopped in my tracks by a knock at the door.

Who the hell could it be?

Quietly, I make my way over to the small monitor that gives a clear view of anyone standing outside. It takes me a few seconds to realise who the image is showing, but when I do, I let out a small sigh of relief for the first time that morning.

It's Miss Summerhythe.

She'd obviously been worried when I hadn't shown up for school and was here to see what the situation was. The sense of not being completely alone brings a smile to my face and being an adult, it's possible that she may be able to explain what's happening to my mother.

I throw the soup bowl down onto the counter, sloshing tasteless drool onto the surface, and bound over to the keypad by the door.

Then, I stop in my tracks.

Seconds pass.

Why am I delaying? A gut feeling? Instinct? Something's holding me back.

And then it hits me: my grandmother's note.

WHEN ILLNESS COMES, FIND EZRA.

At the time, I had no idea what it meant. Now, illness had come, just as my grandmother had predicted – and her instruction could not have been any clearer.

Seek Ezra.

It was no coincidence that my grandmother introduced me to him at her ascension. There must have been over a hundred guests there that night and she only made a point of introducing me to one of them.

I look closer at Miss Summerhythe and notice she is speaking into an earpiece. I hit the microphone button on our telecom.

"…no sign of her, or her mother. Property appears empty. I'll speak to the neighbours and report back."

With that, she walks away. It suddenly strikes me as odd that the school would send out a classroom teacher in the middle of the day to check on an absent student. Then again, everything else this morning has been far from normal. I'm sure Miss Summerhythe finds it odd too – absences don't happen. I'll explain it all to her when I get a chance, but for now I'll follow my grandmother's advice to the letter…

Even if that means visiting Ezra after nightfall at The Rec.

Chapter Eight

Night has fallen. I've been staring at the monitor for an hour. No one else has come to check up on us – even Miss Summerhythe hasn't returned. Maybe she'll come back in the morning.

Maybe she's still watching from a distance.

It doesn't matter: it's time to leave.

I dig out a peaked cap from the bottom of my wardrobe and tuck as much of my hair under it as I can. My hair is thick, red and tucking it under the hat makes my head seem ridiculously big when I check in the mirror.

If Skyla Pearce could see me now…

Never mind – it's not a fashion statement: tonight is about keeping a low profile.

I'm still not sure about leaving my mother by herself, but this afternoon she's showed no signs of getting any better. Or worse, thankfully. Maybe I should be grateful that she seems stable, but the only thing I know for certain is that somehow my grandmother knew this day would come, and I have to follow her advice.

Peering through the gap into my mother's bedroom, I can see she is still breathing. I don't want to disturb her, so I close the door gently behind me and can only hope she won't get any worse before I return.

One final look into the monitor tells me that the coast is clear and, with a hesitant step, I head out into the night.

My senses ping into life. I feel small against the high walls of our CitiBloc and can hear my footsteps echoing as I walk briskly towards the exit and onto the street. I check behind me to make sure I am not being followed. So far, so good.

Outside, the night air is cool and catches the back of my throat. It takes me back to the Ascension Deck, and to my grandmother, and I pick up speed, spurred on by the thought I am doing the right thing. I have decided to walk, sticking to the side streets as I go. Public transport would have been quicker, and easier, but I can't take the risk of being seen.

As I carry on past Citi-Bloc 9 and approach the outskirts of the Residential Tri-sector, I can't believe how long ago this morning seems. I suppose, more than anything, I'm surprised at how easy I've found it to break the rules. Don't get me wrong, I'm not perfect, but in The Panaceum bending the rules is almost unheard of. So far today, I have *broken* several of them. Tonight, I'll be breaking one more. Under 18s are strictly forbidden from going to The Rec at this hour. This is not a warning – it's the law.

Oh well, we can add that one to the list.

I hear The Rec before I see it: low bass sounds thumping in the distance like giants' footsteps. I lower my head, but don't break my stride. I've come too far to back out now. I approach the crest of a hill, and suddenly posters about healthy living, upcoming Government elections, and Nomarks are replaced with colourful adverts for nightclubs and parties. I have now crossed the border between The

Residential and Recreational Tri-sectors...I'm *officially* breaking the law.

On the other side of the hill, I see the back of two imposing buildings, silhouetted by the pulsing red-orange glow that I've come to associate with The Rec. I am close now. Between the two buildings, a shaft of light spills out into the darkness. An alleyway. I head straight towards it, not knowing what scenes will await me on the other side. As I approach, my face is hit by a wall of sound and heat, which I power through with gritted teeth, beyond the safety of the alleyway and out into...

Chaos.

Before I even have time to blink, I am swept along with the surge of the crowd. My feet barely touch the floor as I reach out for an arm, a piece of clothing, *anything* to steady myself. The noise is deafening – an assault of clashing musical styles fighting in the air, and wild screams of excitement from all angles.

As I continue to struggle against the crowd, I catch glimpses of nightmarish images that attack my senses. Fire-breathing clowns, some on stilts, laugh maniacally as they wade through the heaving masses. Doll-like women, with exploded boobs and lips, and heavily painted faces, hand out flyers to groping punters. I can see devils, priests, pigs, nurses, monsters, all thrown together in one huge cauldron of drunken ecstasy.

This is a different world; it's not hard to see why people my age aren't allowed here after dark. By day, I can easily find my way around these streets, but right now I have no idea which direction I am even heading in. Besides, I'm not tall for my age, and can barely see above the people around me. There is no way I will spot Lazer Ink from here.

Suddenly, the crowd surges past a small opening between two buildings and I manage to stumble into it. It feels good to catch my breath, but there is no time to waste. I look around for something to stand on so that I can see over the crowd and get a better sense of where I am. There is a plastic crate not far from where I'm stood, which I quickly turn over and climb on to gain a better vantage point.

"What you up to then?"

The voice comes from the darkness behind me and takes me completely by surprise. I almost fall from the crate.

"Careful, missy! Wouldn't want you to hurt yourself, would we?"

A man of about thirty, with wide eyes and a toothy grin staggers towards me. I freeze as he moves up close enough that I can feel his warm, acrid breath upon my face. I lower my head so that the peak of my cap acts as a barrier to the overpowering stench.

"What's your name then?" he says, swaying gently from one foot to the other. I want to tell him to mind his own business, but that doesn't seem like a good idea, so I settle for a cold silence.

"Oh, come on, I'm not gonna hurt you. Don't hide, I bet you've got a pretty face…"

I feel him grab the brim of my cap and, before I can stop myself, I slap him hard across the face. A shocked grunt of pain tells me that I have done some damage, but I don't wait around long enough to find out. Without thinking, I jump from the crate and throw myself back into the wave of the crowd. This time, I stay low, using my small frame as an advantage as I weave between thrusting bodies and navigate my way. Behind me, I hear a disturbance – my friend must be following me. Luckily, just before I was interrupted on the crate, I managed to spot the neon sign for Lazer Ink a few hundred feet away on the other side of the street.

I push hard. There are a few shouts of annoyance, but I am gone before anyone can do anything about it. I sense that I'm still being followed but turning back to check may be all it takes for me to be caught, so I press on. Finally, the glow of Lazer Ink appears on my left, and after a frantic scramble, I almost fall through the door and slam it behind me. Exhaling loudly, I turn to look through the window, desperately trying to see if I'm still being followed.

Looks like I lost him.

"Ezra!" I call, turning. "It's my mother…"

Ezra simply holds up a hand, demanding my silence. I realise that someone is sitting in the chair and stop, instantly, in my tracks. A client rises, having recently been marked.

"Once that heals, we can move onto stage three, and apply some of the finishing touches. Now, if you'd excuse me," Ezra says with a smile, gesturing towards me as if I'm a problem he needs to attend to.

The client looks into a nearby mirror and admires Ezra's handiwork, before saying goodbye and leaving. Ezra follows the man to the door and looks out into the crowd. I watch on in silence, as he locks the door calmly, and turns to face me. I won't speak out of turn this time, although I'm desperate to explain the reason for my visit.

I soon realise that there is no need.

"Miss Conners," Ezra says, in a familiar, smooth tone, "you're here sooner than we'd hoped."

Chapter Nine

"Take a seat," Ezra instructs, as we enter a small studio space below the shop. Walking down the narrow stairs towards the basement, I'd felt uneasy, but now I stand in amazement. My eyes adjust to the dimly lit space, and I notice every surface is strewn with piles and piles of sketches – hand-drawn designs – on paper that can only have been imported from beyond The Panaceum. I've never seen so much of it in one place; it must have cost a small fortune. Above ground, the designs are displayed on wall-to-wall media screens in vivid, digitised colours. Here, it's as though I've stepped back in time.

I stand in awe.

"Sorry about the mess," Ezra continues as he throws aside a pile of papers revealing an old wooden chair. I sit down, eager to get on with things. I clear my throat as I wonder where to begin, but before I can speak, Ezra interrupts.

"Would you like some tea?"

Tea!? Ezra clearly senses my exasperation…

"Even in times of great crisis, one must always find time for tea."

With that, he turns to a small table and begins preparing two cups. I shift around in my chair, restlessly waiting for his attention. I sigh to show my impatience, but he shows no signs of rushing as he meticulously measures out loose tealeaves with surgical precision. Maybe I really have stepped back in time...

After what seems like an age, my unwanted tea finally arrives, and I take a small sip to appear thankful for it. Grudgingly, I have to admit it tastes delicious.

"You see? Better already, eh?"

I may feel better, but the situation has not changed; I came here for a reason. I have no idea where to begin. I've only spoken to this man once in my life. Can I even trust him?

My grandmother trusted him.

I get to the point. Fast.

"My mother – she's ill."

Now, there's no turning back.

During the five minutes it takes to describe the events of today, Ezra looks at me intently, barely taking time to blink. Mention of my mother's illness, her fit, my grandmother's note, of school and work checking up on us, seem to have no effect on him. He sits, unflinching, except for taking regular sips of tea.

When I am finished, we sit in silence as he appears to process the story, and all of its detail.

"I would like to see the note, if I may. Do you have it?"

A little confused, I pull the note out from my pocket and hand it over. Ezra looks at the handwriting, before picking up a small, pen-like object from a nearby bench. Before I know what is happening, it glows red at one end, burning the paper which quickly turns into little more than black dust upon the floor.

"No!" I yell.

It is the final memory I have of my grandmother.

"It has served its purpose," Ezra explains, calmly. "Now it would only serve to trip us up."

I don't fully understand, but something in his voice assures me that we're on the same team. I nod in acceptance of what he has done as he begins pacing, slowly. For the first time, his brow furrows as if he is searching for what he is about to say or, perhaps how he is going to say it.

"Your grandmother is an astonishing woman," Ezra begins, tentatively. "She would be very proud that you ventured here alone – it must be an intimidating place for one so young. As I said earlier, it is a shame you find yourself here so soon. I'm sure Ida would have loved to have had this conversation with you herself before her ascension, but we prefer not to divulge such information until a child turns sixteen wherever possible. That is, of course, unless it becomes…necessary. Before I continue, I must have your assurance that what I say tonight will, under no circumstances, go any further."

Thoughts fizz around in my brain like fireworks ready to explode from my mouth, but I mustn't speak. I don't dare to distract Ezra from what he is about to tell me.

I nod my head slowly.

Rather than continuing, Ezra silently removes his jacket. Beneath it he wears a plain, black vest, which exposes his bare arms and their rich tapestry of marks. Again, I'm amazed by the thousands of individual designs which seem to be expertly interwoven to create one huge work of art. Most strikingly, on the upper left arm, Ezra's Panacea mark glows, crimson and proud. For the first time, I notice it is inset into a curious design that makes it appear to be the centre of an ornate eye.

"This is the Eye of Horus, or the 'all-seeing eye'," Ezra explains, catching my gaze. "It is a symbol from what many call the *Old World*. I, however, prefer to call it by its less dramatic title: 'the past', as it is, of course, the same world we have always had – even if it may appear very different."

I cannot hide my impatience in wondering where this is going and, thankfully, Ezra senses this and quickens his pace.

"The symbol pokes fun at the notion that some things remain best hidden in plain sight."

With that, he approaches me, taking my hand. Carefully, Ezra places my fingertips over the skin where his Panacea mark lies. The skin is smooth as I trace my fingers around the scar tissue which, for Ezra, serves as the iris of the eye.

"A perfect heal," I whisper.

"Indeed."

"I –"

"Yes, I know. You have one. You will find that your mother has one too."

For the first time, I realise I'd never thought to ask.

"Except, 'perfect heals'…" Ezra begins, looking pained now, reluctant to say any more.

Finally, he relents, "…Do not exist."

"What?"

My brain floods with a whole wave of thoughts that I struggle to make sense of. I glare at Ezra, hoping I have misheard him, but he nods his head in firm assurance.

"Perfect heals do not exist."

I can't seem to make sense of it all, or maybe I just don't want to, because suddenly the answer is everywhere I turn.

Can it really be that simple?

Piled upon the benches...
On paper from beyond The Panaceum...
Tattoos.

Chapter Ten

I'm a Nomark.

The more I think about it, the more I realise there is no other explanation. Sure enough, Ezra confirms my fears.

"The first thing you must understand is that it is not a badge of shame. It's a simple matter of choice – a different way of living."

I begin to feel light-headed. It's too much to take in all at once. First Ezra tells me I'm a Nomark, and then acts as if it's all okay? How can it be okay? I've seen the posters, the videos, the warnings: Nomarks are intruders, Anti-vaxxers are a direct threat to The Panaceum and must be stopped at all costs.

And I'm *one of them*.

I'm the threat.

I'm the enemy…and nobody even told me.

My surprise begins to turn to frustration and anger. To think, I've been living my life without knowing that any day I could be singled out and punished for something I had no idea about?

I rise to my feet, realising that all the while I've had my right hand over my Panacea mark, which I now know is just another of Ezra's designs. Only minutes earlier, it was a sign that I belonged, that I was protected from the diseases that plagued the Old World...now it means nothing. And my mother must have known all along.

"If you would care to hear me out, there's a lot to explain," Ezra says, sensing my agitation.

"I can't be here. I need to be sure."

The words have barely left my lips before I bolt towards the door, darting back up the stairs towards the street.

This time, I hardly even notice the crowd as I burst through it, before rushing over the hill, past Citi-Blocs 9 and 8 – by which point I can hear my heart beating frantically in my ears – and back to Citi-Bloc 7. I ride the lift up to our floor, slap my hand onto the scanner which grants me entry to our hub and lunge through the door to my mother's bedroom. The air seems thick and stale, and low rasping breaths come from the bed where my mother lies, unmoved since I left. I crouch beside her and take her arm from under the covers. Her temperature is still raging, but it barely registers as my eyes dart quickly to her mark. I'd seen it a thousand times before, but now, even without touching it, I know.

The truth hidden in plain sight.

I wish I'd known sooner; maybe we could have stopped things getting this far. Perhaps if we'd been closer, or talked more, or spent more time together...

I should have made time. I should have known.

"Keeping things from those we love is the hardest burden to bear."

Startled, I turn to find Ezra standing in the doorway. There is so much I want to ask him, so much I'm desperate to know, but the events of the day seem to suddenly begin to sink in all at once. I am unbearably tired, confused, and worst of all – with my grandmother gone, a father I'd never really known, and now my mother in such a sorry state – I am on my own. Completely alone.

I sit, nursing my mother's arm as salt tears trickle from my eyes and down my cheeks until I can taste them upon my lips. Ezra stands by, silently, not attempting to console me or comfort me as I sob gently.

Minutes seem to float by, after which, I open my eyes and although I am still tired, confused, and alone, my emotions seem a little less overwhelming than they had only moments earlier.

I am thankful for the release. Now that my mind seems clearer, I think back to what has brought me to this point and begin to remember my conversation with Ezra at Lazer Ink with a more level head. I am ready to know more.

"You mentioned a choice. Earlier. You said that being a Nomark was just a choice. What did you mean?"

I look to Ezra, who has not moved from the spot in the doorway where he has been stood throughout.

"May I?" Ezra asks, motioning with his hand.

I nod, giving him permission to enter the room, but rather than heading towards the chair on the far wall as I expect, he simply sits by me on the floor beside my mother's bed.

"Many years ago, the world was an angry place, where the most powerful currency was fear. A string of long and fruitless wars had left society on its knees, and things were about to get even worse. A *New Plague* swept across to globe, ravaging the population of every country that crossed its path. The United Kingdom got wind of the coming plague shortly before it reached our shores. A selfishness had gripped the people, and most decided to fend for themselves and their families. However, a small faction of like-minded people decided to escape the overcrowded cities and set up a refuge where they might escape the passing of the *New Plague*. Among the group were some of the most brilliant minds of their time: doctors, engineers, teachers, all striving for survival. For months they toiled, with little food or water as they aimed to keep a small area sanitised and disease free. A year later, whilst the rest of the country was all but obliterated, the group survived. The area they'd managed to keep sterile was slowly expanded, and a civilisation grew. Years passed, but the threat of disease was always present…"

"Until The Panacea," I interrupt, nodding.

I've heard most of this tale in history class: how these early settlers went on to risk their lives to salvage supplies and technology from the Old World. Eventually, they went far beyond anything they'd ever expected to achieve…

"It was quite extraordinary," Ezra continues. "Only fifty years ago, we were on the brink of possible extinction, then suddenly we were faced with hope of a future. The dawn of a new age for humankind: The Age of The Panacea. However, not everyone was convinced with this new 'miracle' vaccine."

"Why would anyone choose *not* to have it?" I ask, unable to understand who in their right mind would turn down the chance of sixty years of healthy life.

"Well, at the time, the science was unproven. Yes, too many people were dying prematurely in their thirties or forties after being exposed to the *New Plague*, but those who managed to avoid it were living into their nineties and beyond. People questioned what happened beyond this sixty-year guarantee and the council of the time could not, or would not, give concrete answers – to this day, they still won't. Then there was the concept of 'Heaven'…"

My thoughts immediately turn to my grandmother – where she is, how she is doing, and how I would give anything to have her at my side right now. I begin to understand how the choice may not have been as straightforward as it seemed.

"Despite people's doubts," Ezra continues, "the vast majority of people chose The Panacea. It was understandable, many families had witnessed loved ones die in painful suffering, and the prospect of a sixty-year guarantee put to bed any fears of what might happen beyond those years. Those who were vaccinated became known as Panaceans; those few that remained unvaccinated were to become the victims of a different type of threat altogether."

"A new disease?"

"No."

Ezra shakes his head, ruefully.

"Betrayal."

Chapter Eleven

"You were thrown out?"

"Yes. Little did we know at the time that choosing not to accept The Panacea was a ticket to banishment from our home. Perhaps we were naïve to think that we could share the sanctuary we'd helped to build, but the newly formed Panacean Council said it had a duty to protect fellow Panaceans, and those who were unvaccinated could harbour new strains of viruses that could be a direct threat. Of course, that argument is flawed, but fear is a powerful weapon. As we were so severely outnumbered, the time came when we had no choice but to leave."

A sadness seems etched into Ezra's face beneath all the intricate designs.

"We travelled for days, through a world that was very different from the one we'd left behind. Barren. Empty. The plague had torn through everything in its path. Having little left to feed on, its force had subsided, but we still lost many lives as people were driven – through hunger and thirst – to die at the hands of contaminated food and water. Eventually, the few that remained reached what was once London."

I think back to my grandmother's map of *The United Kingdom*, and its emboldened cities – London is still out there somewhere.

"We forged a lowly life for ourselves – scavenging food and resources like animals – sleeping in filth and squalor. But we survived. Just. We adapted to this new place, learning to live in the much-changed landscape of London, but our quality of life was poor. Some of us had been forced to leave family and close friends in The Panaceum, and we lived in constant fear of disease. Then…"

Even though we are alone, Ezra lowers his voice until he is barely audible.

"Then, around twenty years ago, one of our group found a way back into The Panaceum. Once we knew it was possible, and we could come and go with relative ease, we formulated a plan. Slowly, one by one, a few members of our group infiltrated Panacean society. Our thinking was simple: we could prove to The Panaceum that we were able to live alongside one-another, by actually *doing* so, right under their noses."

"What do you mean?"

"I mean, live secretly within The Panaceum until a set date when we would eventually reveal our presence. By that point, we hoped to have so many of us embedded in society that it would be almost impossible to separate the two. And why should they? If they'd already been living side by side for decades? All we needed were a few brave souls, and someone who could create the believable illusion of a Panacea mark…"

"And that's where you came in," I say, putting the pieces together. I have to admit that even now, knowing what I know, my mother's Panacea mark looks scarily real from no further than a few inches away. Something is still bothering me though.

"My mother is ill. Do all Nomarks get ill?"

"Well, Nomarks – as they've become known in The Panaceum – have the potential to fall ill, yes. Of course, this has no effect on Panaceans, but for now we must keep it hidden whilst our presence remains a secret. We have become very adept at treating illnesses and transporting medications from outside of The Panaceum…"

"So we can help my mother?"

Ezra falls silent. Seconds pass.

"Recently," he begins, "you may have noticed a number of posters, and council notices warning of the threat of Nomarks or Anti-vaxxers."

I think back to Citi-Bloc 1, and the first poster that I'd noticed on the subject.

SAY 'NO' TO NOMARKS. SYMPATHISERS WILL BE PROSECUTED.

At the time, it had seemed strange, but little did I know how much it would come back to haunt me. I nod warily as Ezra continues, "A few months ago, our passage in and out of The Panaceum was discovered, alerting the council to the possibility of outsiders existing within. Since then, a campaign of hate has begun, ordering people to be more vigilant. To begin with, we were branded 'Nomarks', because we were simply unvaccinated. Soon, we were dubbed 'Anti-vaxxers' – pitted *against* The Panaceum. We'd been made the enemy – even though we have nothing at all against those who chose The Panacea all those years ago. We simply want our lives back."

Suddenly, my mother stirs with a huge intake of air. I rush to her side, fearing another fit, but she settles back into her pillow. Ezra joins me, his eyes scanning her body. With an experienced touch, he methodically places his hand upon her cheek, her wrist, and opens up her eyes to inspect her pupils.

"Her temperature is high, her pulse is steady and her vital signs are good," Ezra says confidently, "But how long has her neck been like this?"

In all the chaos, I hadn't noticed that my mother's neck is bulging below her chin, clearly swollen.

"I'm not sure." I stagger. "It can't have been like that before I left, or I would have noticed!"

I think back through the day, trying desperately to recall something I might have missed, but my memory is a hazy wash of events that I can barely make any sense of.

"I have an idea of what we may be dealing with. If I'm right, we'll need medication, and quickly. We'll need to contact London," Ezra says slowly, in an even tone.

"But how will it get here? The escape route's blocked!"

"There may be another way. First, we need to get your mother out of here before the authorities come looking. She's missed a full day of work, unauthorised. Hopefully, she's not already under surveillance. If we're quick, we may be able to get her back to my hub unnoticed."

As he says the words, he is already pulling back the bedsheets and supporting my mother up to a sitting position. With little concern for her modesty, I pass him a nearby night dress which he slips over her head.

"And then you can contact London?" I ask eagerly, as I help him get my mother to her feet.

"No. All communication is blocked. However, there may be a way to get out on foot…"

"But how will you do that?"

As we make our way from the bedroom towards the door, supporting my mother's weight, Ezra picks up speed. Still, his words are crystal clear.

"I won't…" he says, "*you* will."

Chapter Twelve

No sooner have the lift doors opened than we are rushing, wordlessly along a dimly lit avenue towards what I assume is Ezra's hub. All avenues are designed to look the same, so apart from the feeling of being somewhere new, I could easily be anywhere in Citi-Bloc 7.

We reach Ezra's hub, and much like the avenue itself, the layout is familiar. The first thing that strikes me is that the room looks very…normal. The basement of Lazer Ink was like a different world, but here at home, Ezra's hub was like that of any other Panacean – clean, neat, practical.

"Through here," Ezra commands, making his way to what is usually the second bedroom in a hub.

Before Ezra even calls for light, I know that I am now somewhere entirely different from the main living space. The air seems thicker somehow, and smells of something familiar: my grandmother rifling through that old box…me, carefully unfolding the worn, ageing paper in my hands…the map of The United Kingdom.

"Intellihub L-5. Confirm," Ezra calls.

As the lights fade up, I can see that we are standing in a room with walls crammed floor to ceiling with books. Actual books. I have only ever seen a few in my lifetime, and never as many in one place, but here they are – in endless colours and sizes, and fonts. I stand in amazement, scanning titles...

War and Peace...The Lion, the Witch and the Wardrobe...A Brief History of Time...The Complete Works of William Shakespeare...

I turn to find Ezra lowering my mother into a large chair, and quickly divert my attention away from the books in order to help him. I prop her head against a cushion, trying to make her as comfortable as possible. Her neck pulses lightly, looking even more swollen. An arm gently brushes me aside and before I realise what is happening, Ezra places a thin, glass tube inside my mother's mouth. There are numbers and a series of lines on the tube, and as seconds pass a redness begin to make its way towards Ezra's fingers. Once it stops moving, Ezra removes the tube and studies it closely.

"Her temperature is pushing 40 degrees Celsius," Ezra confirms.

I nod, although I don't really understand what that means.

He leaves the room, and quickly returns with dripping towels.

"Wrap two of these around her ankles and hold one against her forehead," Ezra says assertively.

No sooner have I grabbed the towels than Ezra begins searching frantically through a stack of books not far from where we are sat. He rifles through pages, mumbling quietly to himself. All the while, I hold the towel tight to my mother's forehead. Then, Ezra leans forward sharply and pulls open her jaw and peers into her mouth. I catch a glimpse of unusual, greyish patches lining the walls of her cheeks and throat. Ezra sighs.

"What is it?"

"I can't be 100% certain, but I believe it's diphtheria."

Like most things today, this makes little sense to me.

"It's a bacterial disease. Curable," Ezra continues, "but highly contagious. We'll need antibiotics…enough for three people."

Ezra's face is sullen. It doesn't take long for me to realise what he is implying.

"Time is short. You may have a few days before any symptoms begin to appear, or…"

Or, I may not.

I nod, understanding.

"So, come on then, what's the plan?"

Ezra stops in his tracks, looking up – seemingly surprised by my eagerness.

"Spoken like a true Conners," he says with a smile.

I am soon looking at a huge sprawl of pages laid out before me – endless lines, co-ordinates, symbols. The vast web of colours is impossible to process, but I have to soak up as much of it as I can – and fast.

"The sewer system of Oxford was all but abandoned long before The Panaceum was founded. It was one of the first to be hit by rising sea levels and flood zones, leading many to believe the sewers were useless."

"But they're not?"

"Not entirely. I hope."

Ezra leans over and points to a tiny square near the bottom right of the huge grid before us. My eyes follow his finger and rest upon grid reference G4, which contains a faded, red dot and the code T2209A.

"T2209A is a Wastewater Access Chamber, or manhole, outside of The Panaceum which, if my calculations are accurate, still lies above sea level."

He then pulls his finger over towards the top left of the map and comes to a stop on grid reference C12, which holds another dot and the code T2201A. There are hundreds of these dots, many intersected by several lines, which seem to link them all together. I await an explanation.

"T2201A is another manhole which remains above sea level. Look closely."

I lean in for a closer inspection. Beneath this mass of thinner, red lines a single black line runs from T2201A to T2209A.

"The black line represents greater depth, about thirty metres below the smaller, red routes. However, if both entrance points remain above sea level, and the sewer remains intact, then there is a small chance that the passage between those two points is unflooded."

"A small chance? How small?"

"There's no way of knowing," Ezra admits with a shrug, "All we can do is hope."

I look to my mother still struggling for breath.

Hope is enough.

I kiss her on the forehead and look to the door.

"The entrance point – where is it?"

"The south side of Citi-Bloc 1."

"Then what are we waiting for?"

I head for the exit, taking purposeful strides.

"Cressida…"

I stop. No one has called me by my full name for a while – not since my grandmother left.

I turn to find Ezra peeling back a map of the United Kingdom attached to the far wall. Behind, there appears to be a small recess, from which he retrieves a wooden case. His face is sullen.

"There is no way of knowing exactly what you may find down in the sewers or, indeed, what you may encounter on the other side. Whilst The Panaceum may have its flaws, it does protect its residents well from some of dangers that lurk beyond its boundaries. You'll need to be careful…"

With that, Ezra hands over the small case, which I immediately open.

"A gun?"

"Of sorts. This is a LAI gun – a Local Anaesthesia Inductor – which is essentially used by body artists as a nerve blocker to numb areas during particularly painful procedures…"

I'm intrigued to know exactly what type of procedures require nerves to be blocked, but I realise that now is not the time.

"In small doses, its effects are minimal, but turned to its highest setting it has the ability to paralyse a whole limb for a number of minutes."

I begin to piece together what Ezra is implying but he continues cautiously, leaving no room for any confusion.

"In the event that you are being pursued by someone, or something, a shot from this might just give you the window of opportunity you need to escape. Of course, I hope that you'll never have to…"

"I understand."

This is not a game. I look again at the map, trying not to think about what might lie in an underground passage that has potentially been untouched for decades. I exhale and focus in on the route before me.

"And, once I'm out?"

My eyes don't flinch from the map as I try to imprint it upon my brain.

"If you leave tonight, you should reach the far shore by sunrise. The sun will be rising in the East – head towards it. You'll be looking at a walk of at least 8–10 hours, but you'll be able to see The Ether long before you reach it."

"The Ether?"

"Yes. Once our group became more established, we needed to forge an identity for ourselves – create a community. We no longer belonged to The Panaceum, and the jibe of being called Nomarks was a stigma we fought against. We became Etherians, and our home became known as The Ether."

"What does it mean?"

Ezra busies himself, collecting various items from the room and throwing them into a beaten, leather knapsack on the table.

"Cohen will explain everything. He is Sovereign of The Ether – the leader – and you must find him once you arrive. He must be the first to hear the reason for your journey. Trust no one else."

He ties up the knapsack and thrusts it in my direction, before making his way towards the door.

"There are a few essentials in the bag. I will take good care of your mother. Be quick but be safe – we'll be right here when you return. Finally, be careful with those you come into contact with. There's every chance that you are carrying the infection too. Anything else you need to know?"

I have a thousand questions, but one in particular seems to be bothering me more than the rest.

"Why is my grandmother in Heaven?"

Ezra steps back, surprised.

"What do you mean?"

"Well, if we're Nomarks – or Etherians, or whatever – then why was *she* taken to Heaven?"

"Cressida, your grandmother is Panacean."

"But –"

"Look, it's not my place to be explaining all of this."

"Well, if not you, *who*?" I demand, agitated now. "In case you haven't noticed, my mother is seriously ill, my grandmother's gone, I never even *knew* my father before he died, and now the one person who actually has all the answers is telling me that they're not the best person for the job? Just tell me!"

"You'll have to trust me – once you reach The Ether, there is someone in a far better position to tell you everything you want to know…"

"Oh yeah? Who?"

Ezra places a strong, assuring hand on my shoulder.

"Your grandfather."

Chapter Thirteen

It took me twenty minutes just to notice it. It was hardly the grand entrance to a new world; hardly the glamorous start of a heroic quest. How was I to know that it would be hidden amongst the stinking rubbish disposal units at the rear fire exit of Citi-Bloc 1? Yet, here it is – nothing more than a rusted disc on a slime encrusted floor: T2201A.

I look around. The light above the small, metal door of the exit covers the whole area in a pukey green which actually suits the surroundings. The air is thick with the smell of people's rotting leftovers and other household waste, which is being collected in huge metallic containers beneath a series of chutes which run from the flats above.

I crouch down to catch my breath, having run most of the way here.

This place is different at night – Citi-Bloc 1 is alive. The barren streets of my first visit are now filled with commuters making their way to The Rec for work. Gangs of similar-looking men stand beneath streetlights, each trying to be rowdier and more imposing than the next. A scruffy guy at a small stall not far away is urging people to buy energy drinks, and boosters to get them through the long night ahead. I'm tempted, but fear seems to be the only thing I need to keep me alert right now. Even though I've left the main street, I still can't seem to shake off the feeling that I'm being watched. I look up again at the windows above. Nothing. Still, I don't want to be here any longer than necessary.

I squeeze my fingers into the indentations of the manhole cover before me, and heave. No chance: decades of rust and gunk have practically fused the manhole cover to the ground below.

Quickly dumping my bag on the ground beside me, I open it and discover Ezra has packed some snack bars, a bottle of water, the LAI gun, a headlamp, a scarf, some menthol oil and finally…a small crowbar. Perfect. Using one of its pointed edges, I scrape away as much of the grime and rust from the rim and surrounding areas as I can before wedging the bar into an indentation in the lid. I stand upright, and with renewed confidence, I stamp my foot down hard on the crowbar lever I have formed.

Nothing.

In fact, the only thing I *do* succeed in is nearly breaking my foot. It hurts. I think about picking up the crowbar and throwing it as far as I can but, after taking a few seconds to calm down and swallow back the pain, I decide that might not actually be the best idea. I need more leverage though. With my right foot still throbbing, I climb onto the crowbar using a nearby rubbish container to keep my balance. My full weight is now on the bar…but it's still not enough. Doing my best to ignore the pain in my foot, I begin to bounce gently to try and jemmy the lid from the manhole. My bounces gradually get bigger and bigger but deep down I know that it's going to take an almighty force for the cover to even budge. My eyes close tightly as I take off for the final time, launching myself into the air. Using the rubbish container handle, I pull my weight down, and send my feet crunching into the solid iron bar below.

Instantly, it's agony. I crumble to the ground, tensing my whole body in order to try and combat the pain. Excruciating...but worth it. Just before my body hit the ground – just audible above my cry of pain as I dropped to the pavement below – there was definitely a second sound.

Scccchlup!

T2201A was open for the first time in decades.

Peering over the rim, down into the darkness of the hole I'd uncovered, an almost icy chill rises slowly from the depths – but it isn't this which makes me recoil so quickly. The *stench* is overpowering – the thick, rotten smell of dank decay hits me like a wave, forcing me backwards in search of cleaner air. I can taste it; I can feel it clinging to my face like a wet towel, suffocating me. Even from where I now sit, the rising air from the manhole teases at my nostrils. The thought of going anywhere near it again makes my stomach turn and gag reflex rift. All this time, I've been so wrapped up in Ezra's plan that I haven't actually given any thought to what the sewers had been used for in the past...and not only that, but what they'd smell like now, after decades of being sat underground.

I feel sick.

I rise to my feet and take two purposeful strides forward, before once again being forced to my knees, covering my mouth and nose with the fabric from my coat. I'm now genuinely wondering whether I'm going to be able to do this.

But what am I supposed to do? Tell Ezra that I failed, and my mother that I couldn't help her because *the smell was too bad?* No way. I search around desperately for something that might help: bins, the manhole cover, the crowbar…my bag. Is there anything in there? Apart from the water, there are snack bars, the LAI gun, a headlamp, a scarf and some menth…

Menthol oil.

That was it.

Ezra, you genius.

I empty out the contents of my pack and, without hesitation, unravel the scarf and pour onto it several drops of the menthol oil. Then, I gather up both ends and lift it to my face, covering my nose and mouth, before tying it behind my head. My eyes sting as the vapour begins to burn in my nostrils and explode in my skull. Still, it feels like paradise compared to the gut-wrenching pong rising from sewer. Ezra really had thought of everything…

Keen to get moving, I begin throwing items back into my bag, but not before noticing a photograph that I hadn't spotted on my first inspection. The grainy picture is in full colour, but has clearly faded over time. There are four people in the photo. On the right, stands a very young-looking Ezra – there are fewer tattoos, but the style and quality are unmistakeable. Standing beside him is my mother, then my grandmother, both looking youthful. A second man stands behind and has his arms wrapped around the two women. He looks so at ease with them, and there's no question that my mother shares his strong features. It can only be my grandfather. I study the face closely – so familiar despite being a face I've never met. He is also tattooed, but not to the extent of Ezra: under his left eye there are three simple teardrops.

I have so many questions, but the strong smell of menthol brings me back to the task ahead. I close up the bag, and after a final glance over my shoulder...

I descend into the darkness.

Chapter Fourteen

I've been walking for ten minutes – ankle-deep in a century's worth of sludge that doesn't even bear thinking about – when I see the first sign that someone has been here before me. Wading slowly, my torchlight has so far flickered between endless smears of green and brown until a flash of white stops me in my tracks.

IT'S COMING.

The words are crudely sprayed: messy handwriting, or someone in a hurry, panicking? Either way, I don't want to find out. Up to this point, I've been careful – keeping a steady pace and noise to a minimum. Now though, I just want to get out of here as quickly as possible. I push on steadily, figuring that whatever might be down here would be so accustomed to the darkness and the silence that any attempt to be stealthy would be useless anyway. My footsteps echo around the chamber, and I sweep the walls with my torchlight.

The further I get into the tunnel, the more my confidence grows. I've come too far; there's no turning back now, so I increase the pace again. Whilst lost in thoughts of my mother I notice an off-beat between my own steps. At first, I dismiss it as an echo, but it gnaws away at me – my common sense starts to fail, and I start thinking about the graffiti on the wall: What's coming? Who's coming?

BEWARE!

A second warning. I'm panicking now and begin running – but am I heading away from danger or towards it? I'm in the dragon's lair and I can barely see: I am easy prey, but before I know what I am doing, I turn off the torch and stop dead...

Seconds pass.

Nothing.

No footsteps, no monster.

I feel foolish. No sign of any followers behind. Relieved, I turn with renewed determination, flicking the torch back on. And that's when I see it. Cavernous black eyes, gaping mouth, spindle like claws.

THE END IS NIGH – THE PLAGUE CLAIMS ALL

The fragile bones of the skeleton are slumped against the wall surrounded by a few tin cans and a plastic sheet. It's clearly been here for some time – though, whoever it was, their fear was not of any monster, but of the plague. They came here to escape, but there *was* no escape.

Inside The Panaceum, people my age are shielded from death: we see it in films, sometimes, but there is no disease, our elderly are taken away – there *is* no actual death. This is the first time I have encountered it face-to-face. Suddenly, the air feels thick, my lungs contract, the walls seem to close in around me and...

I sprint.

I sprint so fast that if I fall, I will do serious damage but I don't care. I can't spend a second more in here than I absolutely have to. Just as I'm certain the darkness is about to swallow me up, a light appears. It begins as a tiny speck – just like my first sight of life beyond The Panaceum up on the Ascension Deck. Back then, it seemed a million miles away. I had no idea that someday, I'd be risking everything to get there – to the place that my own family once called home.

I'm almost there; the light growing and growing, and the thought of breathing in the cool night air propels me onwards. Finally, I launch myself from the mouth of the sewer and, before my feet even hit the ground, I tear the scarf from my face and take in the pure air in huge, thirsty gulps.

Nothing could possibly feel this good.

I fall to the ground, facing the stars, bathing in the freshness of the moonlit night. I shut my eyes. I could be anywhere: on top of a mountain, under a waterfall – just a moment of peace. Then, even through my eyelids, I sense the light change. A cloud passing across the moon, perhaps? Or a shadow…

"Seems like you've come a long way, young one," says the voice. "Must be mighty important – dangerous place for someone your age to be on your own."

And before I know what's happening, I'm being pulled to my feet.

Chapter Fifteen

We're hovering, perhaps twenty feet in the air, keeping a steady speed in what I can only describe as a huge, mechanical, winged spider – its vast legs reaching out into the night.

"Good thing I found you when I did. Place can be a real maze – even in daylight."

I smile weakly, then nearly jump from my seat when one of the huge mechanical limbs exhales a loud plume of steam as a piston-like leg lurches up by my window.

"Gotta keep the damned things clean if you want a good harvest."

I look on as the scrawny man operating this giant beast pulls a succession of cords and levers, each seeming to correspond with a jagged movement from the mighty machine surrounding us.

"'Course these days, harvesters like this can do most work on auto, but me – I still like doing things myself."

I look out into the night but can see no sign of fields or vegetation.

"What...what do you harvest?" I finally manage.

"You really are a city girl."

I try my best not to look offended.

"The *light,* my dear. We harvest the light."

With that, the scrawny harvester flicks a nearby switch and the ground beneath us is bathed in stark floodlight. There, in countless rows as far as the eye can see in any direction, are masses of solar panels – an army of gleaming soldiers.

"So, your turn…"

"Eh?"

"Well, you know why I'm here: what about you?"

I shift uncomfortably in my seat, I should have known this question was coming. I tense up, but before I know it, I'm suddenly reeling off an utterly fantastical yet completely convincing lie. And – what's more – he's actually buying it. He's nodding his head as I explain to him about escaping from a pack of bullies – led by my nemesis, Kenzi Verhoff – down a manhole somewhere in the back alleys of Citi-Bloc 1.

To my surprise, I'm a natural-born liar.

"Well, sounds like you've had quite a night. Let's get you some supper while we think about how to get you home, your folks'll be worried sick."

"Oh yeah, my dad'll have a search party organised already," I lie – again.

With that, the mechanical washing spider grinds to a jerking halt outside a simple shack, throwing my heart into my ribcage as it does so. The beaten down structure looks nothing like you'd find anywhere in The Panaceum. It's wooden, for a start, and the warm glow beyond the painted timber window frames looks inviting.

"Welcome to my humble home."

We enter a narrow hallway and the Harvester switches on the light – manually. Patterned paper lines the walls as we make our way towards the rear of the building and into a small room, complete with an old-looking sofa and a small side table.

"No use trying to get you home tonight – there are things lurking around out there that you wouldn't want to bump into, believe me. Better off getting some rest and heading out at first light. You must be hungry. I'll fix you some supper. Make yourself at home. Chase here'll keep you company, won't you, boy? Don't let the old man fool you, he can run rings around the rest of us – sometimes disappears for days out there, chasing who knows what? Lord knows where he gets to."

The Harvester then disappears from the doorway, only to be replaced by a shabby, old, grey and white dog. His stooped shoulders give him a world-weary look, but the glint in his eye seems to defy his age – as does the ball which he expectantly drops at my feet. Hesitantly, I pick it up, my palm immediately met with slimy drool which, at first, is sort of gross, but after my twentieth throw, I have to admit, I begin to enjoy.

Just as I'm about to prepare for my *twenty-first* throw, the smell of hearty food fills the room. My stomach yearns loudly for it, and I realise that I can't actually remember the last time I ate anything. The stew looks simple but smells delicious, not that Chase seems to realise as he nudges the ball against my feet in a bid to get me to continue with his game.

"He'll be there for hours if you let him," says the Harvester through a grin. I smile back at him, and as he returns to the main body of the house I kick the ball away, hoping to be left to eat in peace. I have barely lifted the spoon before the ball is back at my feet. I kick it again – same result. Frustrated now, I pick up the ball and hurl it towards the doorway. I miss my target and, instead, it bounces off the wall with a *thunk*. Chase however, seems to get the picture this time, as when he retrieves the ball he leaves the room.

Finally, I can enjoy my supper.

I spoon in the first few mouthfuls. It's warm, hearty and satisfying – but not as satisfying as it *should* be. It takes me a few moments to works out why. Is it the food? Is it exhaustion?

Suddenly, it hits me…*thunk*.

The sound that the ball made when it hit the wall – it was odd. This whole place looks as though it's made from wood, yet there was definitely a metallic edge to the sound as the ball rebounded moments earlier.

I scope the room. The décor is homely, if old-fashioned, but what I hadn't noticed before was that there are no windows.

I've now completely lost my appetite.

I rise from the battered sofa and approach the wall opposite. Before I even knock gently, I know exactly what I'm about to hear.

All four walls give out the same metallic ring.

I bolt towards the doorway with every intention of leaving but, as I reach the passageway, I hear a murmured voice coming from deeper within the house. Common sense tells me to head straight to the door without even looking back, but I can't help myself – I need to know if this smiling 'saviour' is actually out to help me. My mother often tells me that I suspect the worst of people – what if I'm wrong and heading out towards greater danger? What if I'm right and…

There's no time.

I'm not far from the source of the murmuring – feet gliding as smoothly and quickly as I dare in the darkness – when I notice a blue hue spilling from a crack in a doorway. As I adjust my eyes to peer into the room, it's clear that this is anything but the 'humble home' that the Harvester had led me to believe. Monitors stacked wall-to-floor show security images of the entire solar farm: mazy rows of solar panelling, the entrance of the house and – most worryingly – the small, windowless, room with the metallic walls...now standing empty.

I can do nothing but hope that the Harvester's eyes don't fall upon that particular image, on that particular screen. My eyes search around the space as far as the thin opening will allow, but I can see no sign of him. Chase is there, under a desk, nuzzling the rubber ball.

"I can hold her until morning, no problem...I'll be heading back soon to lock it down."

I breathe in sharply as his voice breaks the silence only centimetres away, on the other side of the door. I swallow a gasp as I begin to process what's being said.

"No, we'll need it sooner. First light. She doesn't seem the type to hang around."

He's right about that much.

I shift my weight back onto my heels as I prepare to turn and leave this place for dust, when Chase suddenly looks up from his precious ball and directly at me.

I freeze.

The dog cocks his head to one side before a curious half-yelp, punctuated by the cheery bell of his loose collar, drifts out into the air...

It's enough.

"Damn! I need to go – we have a runner!"

Chapter Sixteen

I've been running for no longer than a minute and already I'm nearly on my knees. It's bitterly cold. It's my first night outside of The Panaceum and away from the protections I'd always taken for granted. I don't belong here, my body hasn't acclimatised, my lungs can't cope, my chest contracts and I'm panicking…I'm really panicking.

I try to calm myself down, but my efforts are broken by the sound of a not-so-distant engine kicking into life.

The Harvester isn't planning to chase me on foot.

I think back to the rows-upon-rows of solar panelling stretching out in all directions as far as the eye can see. Running is pointless – I can't pretend otherwise.

Hide.

I scramble to the nearest bank of moonlit panels, locked tightly together in an unbroken wall, several times my height and sunken into the earth. I glance up, but the surface is steep and sheer – impossible to climb. I look around frantically for anything that might provide some sort of cover. Nothing. And just when I begin to think my luck can't get any worse – *vwoosh* – the whole path before me – *vwoosh* – and everything in it – *vwoosh* – lights up brightly as a summer's day around me. One by one, piercing floodlights with their shocking glare bleach the entire area, exposing me so obviously, that I might as well be an ant on a white tea-plate.

Are you kidding me?

I hadn't spent hours wading through decades of other people's crap to give up on the first night. I lower my chin to my chest, pull the collar of my jacket over my nose and run. I chase the darkness ahead of me, even though every time I draw near it another floodlight illuminates me like a beacon. I switch direction, hoping it may lead to some magical exit but, in truth, I know that I'm doing little more than buying time. I have no idea where I am, or where I'm going – there's no destination. The pointlessness of it all begins to drain the energy from my body. I will my legs to move faster but despite my desperation they seem to be giving up beneath me. Sapped and saddened, I fumble at my bag, hoping to lay my hand upon…*what? A ladder? A jetpack?*

It doesn't matter – because as I swerve around another corner, into yet another avenue of seemingly unending panels, a strong arm locks around my chest, punching the air from my lungs, before the other hand clamps my mouth, stifling a defeated scream. An anguished cry splits the air; my mouth wide, aghast.

But the cry is not mine: I look down at the LAI Gun in my hand, the first of its cartridges now spent. Ezra had been right, at full power, no sooner had the injection hit its target than its anaesthetic properties caused my assailant's vice-grip to loosen entirely.

I spin on the spot, ready to release the second cartridge into the Harvester's head if necessary – but I halt in my tracks. It's not the Harvester: it's a boy – unlike any I've seen – with jet black hair and bronze skin gleaming under the starlight, now groaning, doubled-over in pain. Firmly under the LAI gun's affect, his body sways and dances like a charmed snake, before he drops to the earth, rebounds instinctively to his feet and continues to struggle to keep his body upright as he shifts from one foot to the other. Loose limbed and lethargic, he struggles, raising a single, quietening finger to his lips. The desperation in his eyes suggests he is about as keen to be discovered by the Harvester as I am, and just as I think about questioning who he is, his eyes roll skyward into the back of his head and once again he is face-down of the hard ground below.

Great. I might have just killed the one person who was trying to save me from this situation.

No – a shallow rise and fall of his back – he's still breathing. It's a start – but now, not only am I being hunted in a maze that seems impossible to escape, but I also have a semi-conscious, dead weight, stranger on my hands.

Vwoosh!

As ever, the area around me is bathed in brilliant light, as if to emphasise exactly how trapped I am. On three sides, the impenetrable walls loom, and in the only other direction, the not-so-distant *chudder* of the Harvester's hover machine gets progressively louder.

Block it out…and think.

I look around.

Walls: 1, 2, 3. Stranger. Sky. Hum of the Harvester.

Again. Walls: 1, 2, 3. Stranger. Sky. Hum of the Harvester.

Again! Walls: 1, 2, 3. Chase.

…Chase?

The dog is stood, head cocked to one side, as though surprised to see us. Believe me, the feeling is mutual. I hadn't noticed him run by, but he can't have sprung from thin air so my eyes flash in all directions for an explanation: they fix on a shadow on the ground directly behind where Chase stands, his tongue lolling through a goofy smile.

Sometimes disappears for days out there…Lord knows where he gets to…

A hole – probably one of many.

The bronze boy by my feet now splutters in the dust as I nudge him with a foot, but a hint of a breeze tells me the huge fans of the hover blades are almost upon us. There's no time for subtlety. I turn the boy over, lean close – he smells distant and pure – before slapping him squarely across the face.

"Whargh…guh…wharra…"

The anaesthetic is still at work.

I press my finger against his lips, hard, and lock my eyes on his. I see the night's stars above reflecting back at me, and I know – I just know, we're on the same team.

"We have to go," I whisper.

He does his best to nod.

"Go on, boy!"

Chase disappears into the tunnelled earth whilst, hip to hip, the bronze stranger and I drag our way towards the unknown.

Chapter Seventeen

"We need to move."

"Well, you should've thought about that before you stabbed me in the leg."

The conversation has continued in this way for at least half an hour. His speech has become gradually less slurred though – the anaesthetic must be wearing off. We've found a place to rest by some water – something between a small pond and a large puddle – which Chase is now happily splodging about in. He clearly isn't reading the atmosphere, as the boy, still bronze under the moonlight, has sat with his back to me with barely a sideways glance ever since we escaped the Harvester.

"For the last time, I didn't *stab* you – I injected you, you're only paralysed."

"Oh, great! Paralysed for how long?"

"I...don't know...but your voice seems to be nearly back to normal again, so it must be wearing off."

"Well, forgive me if I don't jump for joy."

"Listen, I'm not the stalker here. How long have you been following me? If I hadn't dragged you out from those solar panels then you'd still be with the Harvester now, praying for..."

"Jonah."

"What?"

"My name's Jonah. Yours?"

"Cressida. My friends call me Cress."

"I'll remember that…Cressida," he says with a glint in his eye, and I smile despite myself. The tension in the air seems to clear. Jonah turns, and for the first time since we crossed paths, I have a chance to study his face. I am conscious of making him feel uncomfortable but, as I scan its contours, I can see that I am as much of a mystery to him as he is to me. Where my features are fair and rounded, his stand hard and jagged. With copper skin, roughed-up by the environment – a life exposed to the elements – I wonder what he must be thinking of my own comparatively ghostly complexion, untouched by anything outside of The Panaceum. The dark, entwined, hair framing his face so naturally was a long way from the cropped and over-styled trends of home.

"We need to move," I repeat, breaking my own daze.

"I know," he says, "give me your hand."

I do.

It's pretty clear that we're not going anywhere fast. Jonah's speech may have improved since we ditched the Harvester, but any attempt to put his full weight on the affected leg was pointless. Jonah groans, more in frustration than pain and trains his eyes back to the direction of the solar farm.

"He'll find us."

"Who? The Harvester?"

"Harvester?" Jonah repeats, confused.

"Yes – he told me he harvests the light."

"*Machines* harvest the light. He's an operative: a snitch, a guard dog, hired by The Panaceum to collect up any strays like you and make sure that they don't cause trouble."

"How do you know all this?"

"I've watched him. That's what I do."

"So, you *are* a stalker."

"I'm a *scout*," he snaps, his eyes remaining fixed on the same spot in the distance. It's not hard to see now that his vigilance is highly tuned, and his distant responses are down to the fact that our meeting wasn't by chance: he's working.

"Now, are you going to tell me why you were crawling out of a sewer?"

I get the sense that the sarcastic banter of minutes earlier is well and truly over.

"I…can't."

"What?"

"I can't tell you. I promised."

Jonah's eyes slowly creep round to mine.

"Are you kidding me?"

"I said —"

"Said what?"

"I said I'd tell no one but Cohen."

His eyes widen in recognition.

"I was sent here by —"

"By Ezra," Jonah finishes, staring at me, transfixed.

I now have his undivided attention.

*

Five minutes later and Jonah is up to speed – Ezra, tattoos, the LAI gun, Cohen, the plan, the sewer. Everything, except my mother…and the illness – just as I promised Ezra.

He listens intently throughout and, for once, he doesn't interrupt. In fact, even when I finish, he doesn't say a word, taking his time to process my story and, I soon realise, *me*. Then, once my silent interrogation is over, he speaks.

"Show me."

I unzip my jacket and remove my left arm, now bare and cold against the night's chill. Without warning, he reaches towards me and traces the outline of my Panacea Mark. Back in Art class, I'd been looked on as unique, but in the way a person might look upon a quirky sideshow. Now, Jonah's eyes show me complete acceptance, and for the first time that I can remember, I feel I belong to something – even though I've barely scratched its surface.

"You were lucky to have got through the sewer – there was no guarantee it would be safe. That was brave…and stupid."

"I didn't have a choice."

"I believe it. Cohen knew it was one of the few places Ezra might have tried to make contact with the Ether after our regular supply route was discovered. I've been watching it for weeks – as has your 'Harvester'. I followed you to the solar farm, and to his cabin, and I was ready."

"For what?"

"To kill him…if it was necessary. But then you escaped, and I thought I'd lost you in that maze – so I followed the dog."

"Chase?"

By now, Chase is lying asleep, as though this is just another regular night. Something told me I wouldn't be sleeping quite so peacefully.

"So, can you get me to The Ether?"

"Of course – it's where I live. But it's a good day's walk from here, so we'll get some sleep and hope I'm up to the journey by sunlight. We'll keep watch in shifts – hopefully your friend might turn up by morning, but if not then we'll have to leave without her, I'm sorry."

"Um…friend?"

"Yeah – your friend from the sewer. She managed to get out too, just after you got taken away by the Harvester."

My mind races back to the sewer – those distant footsteps. At the time, I'd feared some monster lurking in the dark, but the truth may be just as frightening…

I motion to speak, but it's clear that Jonah is already on my wavelength.

"Get some rest. You'll need it."

"But –"

"Sleep…please."

I read between the lines and this time, I don't protest and close my eyes despite feeling anything but restful.

Minutes pass – maybe I'm even on the brink of sleep – when I feel breath against my cheek. It's Jonah – I can tell.

"Listen carefully, and don't move. Here's what we're going to do…"

Chapter Eighteen

As plans go, it's pretty basic – lay the bait, catch the bad guy – but it's the only option we've got. It's barely sunrise, and I'm walking briskly down a woodland pathway, glancing over my shoulder every now and then – just as instructed. Jonah should be somewhere up ahead. Beside me, Chase trots along unaware of the vital role he is about to play – I just hope he's up to it.

At a fork in the path, I take a right: this is my cue to sprint – we need a gap to lay the bait. Rounding a tight bend, I hurtle on with Chase in tow, until…

"Psssst!"

The signal: Jonah must be set nearby.

I stop and from my pocket quickly produce a morsel of meat, which I lay down on the ground. Chase's eyes light up and he eagerly tucks into the treat, scarcely believing his luck. As he does so, I back away into a nearby bush, ducking down as low as I can.

Now, we wait.

Silence – except for the clacking of Chase's drooling jaws.

Within seconds, faint footsteps approach and finally stop, metres away. A breathless voice.

"Where's your friend gone, boy?"

A woman's voice: one I've heard before, but where? Before I have a chance to think about it, the air is cut by an agonised scream.

"Aaaargh!"

A heavy drop. I rush out and see our pursuer face down in the earth. I raise her head from the floor...

Miss Summerhythe?

She looks nothing like the same strait-laced art teacher who had taught me back in The Panaceum, but there's no doubting it's her. I watch on as she struggles for breath, and notice a large, curved, stick on the ground by her side. It is unlike the other woodland debris, and on closer inspection I can see that it is engraved with pictures depicting an eye, a wheel, a compass...

"Thanks," Jonah interjects, taking the object from me and replacing it in a holster between his shoulder-blades.

"What's *that*?"

"A throw-stick," he replies, as if it's the most natural thing in the world. "We use them for hunting, mainly – but they come in handy for all sorts of things."

"And the engravings?"

"Oh, important dates, life events...each Etherian's throw-stick is unique. Now come on, let's see who we've got here..."

*

Bound and grazed, Summerhythe hasn't said much – and to be honest in the shock of the situation, neither have I. Having held up his end of the bargain and been duly rewarded, we've sent Chase home – towards which, he bounded merrily as if this was just another day at the office.

Now, we're alone with Summerhythe, and I want answers.

"You came to my home...why? Why you?"

Nothing.

"Miss Summerhythe..."

"*Agent* Summerhythe," Jonah interrupts. He's been rummaging through her rucksack and is holding up leather wallet. "She's one of *them*: Agent Clarice Summerhythe, Chief Panacean Council Operative."

"A Chief PCO? No, that can't be right, she's an art teacher at my school. She's been there for years. Why would a teacher..."

And then it clicks: every student, in every year group, passes through her door. And I bet every student has the same lesson; innocently drawing a friend's Panacea Mark. Finding a perfect heal is a big occasion at our school...but Summerhythe isn't there to celebrate us, she's there to *identify* us. Identify the Nomarks.

"You've known for months – have you been spying on me ever since then?"

Nothing. I want to put my boot to her face right then. Jonah must sense my anger, grabbing my arm.

"Not now, Cohen will have plenty of questions for her, and he can decide what we do with her. Let's keep moving. We need to get to the shoreline before nightfall."

He's right – another world awaits us, and the old hierarchy doesn't count for much where we were heading.

"Walk," I bark at our silent captive.

The tone surprises me – I barely recognise my own voice. Twenty-four hours earlier I couldn't have imagined talking to anyone like I'm talking to Summerhythe now, never mind a *teacher*. Yet, despite my command, she remains unmoved.

"I'm going nowhere."

"Fine," Jonah interjects, already beginning to march away, "Stay here. Bound up like that, you'll make a good meal for something (or someone) after nightfall. There are things in these trees that will tear you limb from limb."

I look to my one-time Art Teacher – both of us out of place in this alien landscape – and can't help feeling that I'd rather not see her become a meal, despite not trusting her. Agent Clarice Summerhythe stares back at me, and behind the defiance in her eyes, she cannot hide the undercurrent of fear…much like I can't hide mine.

Without words, we walk, following Jonah further into the unknown.

Chapter Nineteen

"We're not going to make it."

"Well, it would be a lot easier if I could actually see where I was going!"

Jonah had insisted that Summerhythe should been blindfolded for the journey and let's just say, she's less than happy about it.

"I could break my neck!"

"Oh, well we wouldn't want that, would we?" Jonah snipes, with more than a hint of sarcasm.

Summerhythe's voice is lower, and colder than I remember, and I start to wonder: was everything about her teaching persona an act? Either way, throughout the day, she's become more outspoken, to the constant annoyance of Jonah.

"Walk faster."

"I can't."

Jonah doubles back from his advanced position sharply to within millimetres of Summerhythe's ear.

"Look, if it's a choice between us getting to the shoreline by sunset and getting rid of you – I'll get rid of you, and I won't think twice about it. Understand? Now walk."

He shoves her – hard – between the shoulders. Her hands, being bound behind her back, are no help as she loses balance and her face crunches on the woodland floor beneath us. Unswerving, Jonah strides past her and onwards. Summerhythe manages to writhe herself round into a seated position and I find that, despite myself, I offer a hand under her arm and help her to her feet.

"Thank you," she mutters quietly. "Look, I don't have a clue how we got here. We've been walking for hours. If you took the blindfold off, I wouldn't be worried about breaking my neck every step I take, and I'd be able to walk a lot faster."

She has a point.

I take off the blindfold. She catches my eye and smiles, but nothing has changed.

"Don't. We're not friends. Just keep up."

For the next half an hour, we climb gently up slope. The air around us gets colder and colder and a relentless breeze kicks up as dusk draws in. I glance up momentarily to check we're still on course and see that Jonah has stopped walking. All I can see is his silhouette against the sky – whatever slope we've been climbing, *this* is the top. I have no idea what to expect as I approach and stand shoulder to shoulder with him – but the sight takes my breath away. The vast expanse of water, steely grey against the closing darkness stretches out into what seems like an endless horizon. The spray from the lapping water at the shoreline prickles my face. Then, looming amongst the low-lying mist, I can just about make out the hazy outline of a beastly structure with huge arches and interconnected towers…

"The Ether. Quite something, isn't it?" Jonah shouts over the wind.

"It's incredible."

By now, Summerhythe has also reached the summit. It's clear by her face she's as awestruck as I am; myth becoming a reality.

"Come on, if it gets any colder, we'll freeze to death on that water," Jonah warns.

We descend down some makeshift steps cut into the jagged cliff-face, and head towards what I'd assumed from above was a large rock but is, in actual fact, a sheet of canvas. Jonah pulls it back to reveal what looks like some sort of motorcycle without wheels.

"We'll get across using the jet-ski," Jonah says.

My excitement level builds – I have never been on the water before, never mind on anything like this.

"Where do I sit?"

"Oh, there's only one, and I'll be driving. You'll have to keep an eye on Summerhythe. You'll be going in this."

Jonah reveals a small, worn, rubber dinghy – beaten and rough-shod, with more than its fair share of patches. It looks about as seaworthy as an old tyre.

"Come on! Let's tie her on," Jonah yells enthusiastically, "We'll have you towed there in no time."

Chapter Twenty

Th-wump! Another almighty crash as the dinghy lands hard against the swell, sending water pluming high into the air. We're ripping through the tide, launching between one wave and the next, at a thrilling pace. I look ahead to Jonah – he smiles back. Meanwhile, Summerhythe has turned a shade of green behind me – her knuckles gleaming white where she clings to one side of the dinghy's flimsy upright.

"Faster!" I yell at the top of my lungs. Jonah laughs now, and my body jolts as I feel the jet-ski hurtle towards top speed. Summerhythe groans as we are once again thrown into the air, only to land with another boneshaking thud. I regain my balance and feel the tingle of spray on my arms as we race on. The sun is setting, and if it wasn't for the adrenaline buzz coursing through my body, I have a feeling I'd be damned near frozen – but before us, The Ether is ablaze in the dying light. We're close now, and from this distance, I notice that the towering structures before us are interwoven with an intricate web of wires and platforms. It strikes me as odd…until I realise that, before us, the waves simply crash against the face of the buildings – there *is no* ground to speak of. We're not heading towards a shoreline, but rather towards the base of what seems to be one of the tallest towers – a vast, spike-like crack reaching into the sky.

"The Shard!" Jonah yells, clearly reading my inquiring eyes.

As we draw nearer to the imposing structure, the waters become more turbulent, and the confidence I felt out in the open quickly drains away from me. The engine of the jet-ski cuts out, and Jonah dismounts onto a floating jetty, where he secures the vessel with a rope. Next, he hauls-in the dinghy, and offers me an outstretched hand – pulling me up to join him. Now, there's only Summerhythe to contend with – but it seems she has no intention of moving, her vice-grip tightening.

"Come on!" Jonah yells, but Summerhythe is less of a sickly green now as she is a *deathly* grey.

"I'm not moving!"

I sense a stalemate, but Jonah has other ideas, quickly engaging a flick-knife and asserting the pressure of the blade against the moorings – the only thing standing between the dinghy and the open waters.

I have never seen a grown woman move so fast in all my life…

Now, the three of us are standing side-by-side.

"Here, put these on," Jonah yells above the roar of waves.

Summerhythe and I think better of questioning him, and quickly secure the life-jacket-style vests in place.

"I would have appreciated this a lot more when we were *out on the water!*" Summerhythe moans and, to be fair, she has a point.

Just then, a haunting metallic cry rings out.

"Good, he knows we're here."

"Who?"

I notice Jonah is clipping ropes to iron rings on the floor as he answers.

"Big Ben –"

"Big…?"

"The bell – summoning the council elders to The Shard. Someone must have spotted us approaching – we should get going."

My eyes follow Jonah's hands to the clips, along the ropes, to their target: my life jacket.

"Where are we going?"

"The only way we can go…up."

Jonah is now uncoiling a large cable from around a hook. I follow the cable up…up…further than I can even see.

"Hold on tight," he says, grabbing my hand.

And suddenly, my guts are in my boots. We rocket skywards at incredible speed. The platform on which we were standing disappears beneath us as we zoom up the face of the building – bodies winched, legs dangling and nerves shredded.

*

I feel sick.

Jelly-legged, light-headed and with hair that I can only imagine resembles some sort of wild bird's nest, I somehow find myself on top of the tallest building I've ever seen.

I put my hands on my knees for support, breathe deeply, and search for any detail in my hazy surroundings. Slowly, the shapes of people begin to emerge, more – many more – than the two I made my ascent with. One of the figures seems to be approaching me, so I concentrate hard to make out the face. For a second, my heart stops as I swear I see my mother before me, but then three teardrops come into focus on the face – the face of a man I'd seen before, only once, in a photograph…

"Cressida?"

I don't get a chance to respond, as strong arms suddenly envelop me in a warm embrace.

After what seems like an age, he eventually releases me.

"Why are you…how…?"

Every part of me wants to tell this man that his daughter is desperately ill. Surely, he has a right to know? Surely, above Cohen or anyone else, he is the one person I can trust? I see his eyes, imploring me for an answer, but all I can hear are the distant words of Ezra – and he hasn't let me down so far…

"I need to speak to the Sovereign."

"But Cress…" Jonah starts.

"Immediately."

The people around me look on, bewildered by my demand. But my grandfather simply smiles.

"I see Ezra has instructed you well. This is all a lot to take in – let's do this properly. You shall have your meeting: Assemble the Etherian Council," he instructs. "But first, some dry clothes – that sea spray will irritate the skin…especially of one who has been accustomed to The Panaceum as long as you have, my dear."

Chapter Twenty-One

Well, it's a good thing *dirty beige* is my colour…

It turns out the clothes are very different here: but they're dry, and I do feel a lot better after getting out of my old outfit – with all its sewer-stank, and Harvester-chase sweat, and murky sea-water stench. I feel clean now and – dare I say – even *refreshed* as I enter a basic holding room, where Jonah is already waiting. He has fresh clothing too and seems, somehow…

"Well, you look…different," Jonah spouts.

That was the word – different.

"Mm-hm," I reply, giving a mock twirl, "you too. Amazing what a clean face can do for a person."

"Or a hairbush…apparently." He nods, noticing my freshly washed hair.

I grin and turn away as I feel my cheeks getting warm.

Jonah continues, "You do realise that –"

"The council is ready for you now."

Our attention is diverted. A tall figure stands in the doorway dressed head-to-toe in a sleek, black, rubberised material – the style, cut, angles, all as severe as the face of the woman wearing it. *Fierce* would be an understatement.

Without any further ceremony, she leaves and, wide-eyed, I follow.

As Jonah joins me, I whisper, "Hey, when do I get to wear one of *those*?"

"Depends how long you stay. I have a few spares you could borrow."

"Oh yeah, right."

"Seriously! Neoprene. We all have them – keeps out the cold, the water, and the toxins within it. All pretty handy when you live in the middle of the sea. We salvage it from old wetsuits. Some people are just a little more imaginative with it than others. Won't find many frills on mine though."

The severe-looking woman is just ahead now, standing by an open door impatiently; as if I'm somehow late for a meeting that *I* called and wanted to happen *immediately* before I was *ordered* to get dry and change into this shapeless sack. Anyway, I don't want to cause a fuss, so I quicken my step and smile politely as I pass her and enter a room – *Etherian Council Chamber*.

The glassed walls offer a 360-degree view of the Ether which, by night, as I look out, is little more than a blanket of twinkling lights. Suddenly, I'm back on the Ascension Deck, seeing those *same* twinkling lights, wondering about the possibility of life beyond The Panaceum. Except, I'm not: I'm not on the Ascension Deck now, or in The Panaceum, I'm *here*. And while I'm here, I'm going to try to make sense of everything I've always felt has been kept from me in the sheltered 'sanctuary' of home.

I feel Jonah squeeze my hand and look up to find the council members rising to their feet – each donning variations of the sleek, black, neoprene Jonah spoke of. He's right –

whilst the room is awash with black, between them, no two people look the same. My eyes dart from structured collars to asymmetric skirts, ostentatious epaulettes, and a frankly ridiculous decorative headpiece which the person standing next to its owner was thoroughly unimpressed by.

"I told you some people get a little carried away," Jonah mutters, as if tuning into my thoughts.

And it wasn't just their clothes that they seemingly got carried away with. I have never seen so many people in one room with so many marks: hands, necks and faces – anywhere that wasn't covered by neoprene – bore a strikingly different set of designs. It was fascinating. A bell chimes from afar, and quickly all attention is diverted to an unoccupied chair at the head of the room; I brace myself, assuming we're about to be introduced to the Sovereign of The Ether. The lights around me dim, as a hooded entourage enters from behind the chair – the leader of which carries a flaming sceptre. They head towards the centre of the room where, between the two seating banks, a rustic steel grill stands aloft on a bronze podium emblazoned with the words: "We withstand, we adapt, we succeed. Our light will endure."

The flames from the sceptre dance on the dimly lit faces of the councillors as it is purposefully lowered towards the grill. Instantly the fuel ignites, engulfing the surrounding oxygen and sending light flaring into the atmosphere. The hooded faces are suddenly ablaze in firelight, and I feel my jaw drop to the floor.

It can't be…?

But there they are, those three little teardrops.

The entourage departs, leaving the leader – the Sovereign – to take their position at the head of the room before placing the sceptre, still alight, into a holster. The room returns to its normal state.

A booming voice reverberates around the chamber.

"This hereby opens the 873rd sitting of the Etherian Council, as requested by one Cressida Connors. Be seated."

Instantly, the room sits in unison: unsurprising, as the gravity in the voice is so weighty that even *I* feel I should sit despite not actually having a chair. I stand stiff-limbed, eyes transfixed by 'The Sovereign'.

"You have the floor, Cressida."

Well, I got what I asked for – I have their full attention – but they're all so old and important-looking and I'm…dragging this out. It's just hard to believe that the man before me – commanding the respect from the entire room, ruling over proceedings – is the same person who was weeping into my hair and embracing me so warmly on the rooftop less than an hour earlier. And how will it be possible to tell this man – my grandfather – in front of all these strangers, that my mother, his *daughter* is…

Quit stalling. My mother could be dying.

I bite down hard on my lip.

"Take all the time you need," I hear.

But there *is no* time.

"My name is Cressida Connors."

Murmurs within the crowd.

"I have travelled from The Panaceum…"

Louder now.

"…and my mother is desperately ill."

107

Chapter Twenty-Two

Eighty-seven. Eighty-seven eyes have glared at me, unflinching – except for the briefest sideways glance to a neighbour – for the past five minutes.

Yes, eighty-seven…one lady is wearing a patch.

Their eyes widened when I mentioned my mother's illness, the new escape route from The Panaceum, and my (numerous) near-death experiences. Their faces softened at mentions of Ezra, my mother and my grandmother.

Jonah, meanwhile, has gawped at me the whole time, open-mouthed, like a landed fish. I feel sorry that I haven't been able to tell him any of this earlier. I've wanted to. Well – time will tell if he resents me for not trusting him. If he knows me at all, he'll understand it was for a good reason.

And my grandfather…well, I didn't dare make eye-contact with him at all as I delivered the stinging news, for fear that I wouldn't be able to reach the end of the story myself. I'd had days, or at least hours, to cope with it all in private. My grandfather was hearing it all at once, for the first time – and in the most public of forums.

I finally look at him, and immediately see each emotion within the micro expressions of his face: Pain. Love. Relief. Anguish. It's a face I've known for so little time but can read as clearly as I can my own mother's. He's on the edge – fear swelling, surging towards the surface. I don't break his gaze: I give him my strength and urge him to action.

I got here. I did my part...now it's time for you to do yours.

"And you, Cressida. You're feeling...?" he manages.

"Fine. I feel fine. No signs yet."

"Good. Very well – you will remain here with me tonight. Then at daybreak, a party will escort you to the medical facility whereupon the appropriate treatment will be –"

"Sovereign Cohen."

A nervous fidgeting ripples through the crowd. Bodies turn to get a better view of a tall, bearded man – plainly suited, thick-shouldered and standing stock still among the surrounding commotion as if rooted to the ground. He appears at home with the attention he's receiving.

"Whilst I naturally respect the sensitivity of the situation, Sovereign, there is a clear conflict of interest at play here. Ms Connors, despite her lineage, should quite clearly remain in isolation until we can administer the appropriate antitoxin, and until such a time as we are satisfied that she poses no risk."

"My granddaughter will not be subject to clinical isolation after such an arduous journey."

Silence – lingering and oppressive. The air becomes heavier as every nanosecond trudges by and the audience await who will dare to speak next.

"Again, with respect, Sovereign Cohen, our hearts must not be allowed to guide our heads here. We have no guarantee that we're actually dealing with diphtheria! It could be something much worse. A diagnosis that Ally Ezra has determined from a *book* is not reason to —"

"Ally Jofra, please. Let me be clear. I trust Ally Ezra more than most. I trust him with my life: I trusted him with my granddaughter's life, and I trust him with…my daughter."

The word 'daughter' breaks in his throat.

Jofra softens the approach.

"All I am highlighting is that for the sake a simple precaution, we could be facing an outbreak, and we simply don't have the resources."

"She can stay with me."

Oh good – Jonah has now waded into the fray…

"I've accompanied Ms Connors at close quarters for 48 hours. If anyone has been at risk from a contagion, it's me. We'll go straight home and sit tight. She can stay with me tonight – we'll both get checked out tomorrow."

"Even once the treatment is administered, we can't be certain that the toxin —"

"She can stay with me as long as it takes. Okay?"

Both parties seem appeased – neither one happy, but neither having lost or won the battle. I quietly allow myself to grin at Jonah referring to me as 'Ms Connors'. Suddenly, a thought hits me.

"What about her?"

Summerhythe, all the while, has been closely flanked by two beefy-looking guards who, in addition to the regulation neoprene, also don a breastplate and gauntlet-style gloves that don't give the impression that they are designed for comfort.

"We will isolate Clarice Summerhythe before questioning. She is no longer your concern."

Chapter Twenty-Three

It's quiet – really quiet. There are no vehicles here, no distant bass sounds pulsating from The Rec – no advertising disrupting the night sky – just the waves, gently shushing against the buildings. It's dark, but I have no idea of the time. And it's cold: really cold.

We must have been walking for about twenty minutes with barely a word. The session at the council was a lot to take in – for both of us. Even so, the quietness is starting to get to me now and I'm eager to gauge where Jonah's mind's at about, you know, stuff.

"So, 'Ms Connors', eh? Kinda…formal."

"Yeah, well, don't get used to it," he smirks. "I was at work, remember – you're my *job*."

"Charming."

Back to silence, before.

"So, diphtheria, eh?"

Walked into that one.

"Look, I wanted to say something."

"Forget it. You did the right thing."

Even in the darkness, I can sense that he's not just saying it – he means it.

Above us, I notice small specks of red light at the top of the tallest shadows that loom all around us. I guess they mark the top of buildings. Somewhere below us, and from nowhere, the ground let's out an aching groan, metallic and stretching out over seconds...a beast in the deep.

"You'll get used to it. These old things were never meant to withstand 100 feet of water," says Jonah, looking up at the skyline, unfazed.

Then, he stops.

Before us, there's a huge arc of those same red lights and, as my eyes adjust, I see that they are attached to what appears to be an enormous wheel – the bottom of which lies submerged within the sea below.

"This is your...house?"

"Well, that – that's The London Eye, but yeah...it's where I live."

"Where?"

"The penthouse, of course!"

Jonah cranes his neck skyward and I follow his gaze to the very top of the wheel, hundreds of metres above us.

"Come on," he calls, "let's climb."

"What is it with you and ridiculous heights?" I retort.

"Well, I'm a Scout," he yells, already making his way up a succession of ladders. "It's the best place to, you know, *scout* things."

*

The 'penthouse', as it turns out, is not quite as plush as the title might suggest. That said, there's a raised area in the centre of the oval-shaped 'capsule' piled high with blankets and soft furnishings which, under the warm light of a lantern, looks dreamy compared to last night's camping spot. I see a telescope ('for scouting' of course), maps with coordinates, a few boxes that I can only assume hold some personal belongings, and...not much else, really. Except windows, everywhere – glass on all sides from floor to ceiling – so much so, that if you look directly out to sea, it's easy to imagine you are floating in mid-air which, at this height, seems both amazing and terrifying all at once.

"Good for scouting, I'd imagine," I eventually manage to say, before taking a closer look at the map: its buildings interlinked by lines and bridges, surrounded by sea.

"Yep."

"Seems pretty secure to me. What do you look out for?"

Jonah removes some of the bedding from its platform and forms a makeshift bed at one end of the fairly confined space.

"It's been a long day," he says, making his way back to me for one final look through the telescope. "Rest up. Tomorrow's going to be a big day."

"Am I on the bed, or the floor?"

Jonah smiles as he slowly makes his way back to the far end of the capsule.

"As if there could be any debate...Ms Connors."

Chapter Twenty-Four

"There, that should do it. If you did harbour any of the bacteria, then that should nip it in the bud. Still, I would recommend avoiding close contact with anyone for the next 24–48 hours. Here, hold this over the site in case it bleeds a little."

"Thanks," I say, pressing a cotton pad tight to my arm, which stings where the anti-toxin has been injected. At least the ordeal is over though. Don't get me wrong, needles are fine, but the atmosphere in the treatment room has been painfully awkward ever since Jofra and I had left Jonah and my grandfather outside. In this clinical light, Jofra is not nearly as imposing as he'd appeared at the council meeting last night. He is still tall, and beardy, but the features of his face are softer than I'd expected despite the serious expression he wears…

"Cressida, I feel I ought to apologise for what may have seemed like over-cautious hostility towards you at last night's meeting," Jofra ventures.

"Mm-hmm."

"You see, when one is responsible for the well-being of an entire community – a community that has limited resources, then one –"

"Don't worry about it."

"The last thing we can do is risk an outbreak that —"

"I get it. Don't worry about it."

Jofra nods gratefully, appearing to be relieved that I have cut his rambling apology short. I even smile.

"Good. Well, here are two more doses of anti-toxin, along with additional antibiotics and notes regarding administration and dosage. Your mother and Ezra will need to take both. I'll pop them into this pack."

Laid out on a table beside me is the pack in question, alongside my very own sleek, black, neoprene ensemble. Unlike others I've seen, this one has zero frills – no fashionable cuts, no collars, no extras – just a basic figure-hugging monstrosity that seems designed specifically to highlight every possible insecurity a teenage girl might have. Great.

"I'll give you a few private moments to change, and then feel free to make your way out to the waiting area. Your grandfather is very keen to give you a tour of our facility. I think you'll find what we're doing here very interesting."

*

I emerge minutes later – looking like something between a ninja and a seal – and am surprised to find that Summerhythe has joined Jonah and my grandfather in the waiting area. The suspicion clearly shows on my face, which seems to be matched by Jonah's, and provokes an explanation.

"We have invited Agent Summerhythe along for our tour to shed some light on findings that we sense are being concealed from inhabitants of The Panaceum," says my grandfather.

Well, now I'm intrigued.

Agent Summerhythe doesn't seem thrilled at the prospect. In fact, she seems a little weary after what I'm sure was a fun night of awkward questioning and looks more timid than she has done previously.

We are led down a sterile-looking corridor – you know the type: mostly white, washable surfaces, smells like bleach. The Panaceum's medical facility is much the same: despite having no disease, people still break bones, suffer accidents and, of course, harm each other or themselves...we're still human. I've only been there once or twice, but the ambiance is memorable and, so it appears, universal.

"On your left and right are general treatment rooms and research labs where we are continually attempting to keep on top of any ailments which may affect our citizens. As we approach the far end of the corridor, we reach the quarantine area, where anyone with an unidentified (or untreatable) illness is placed for observation, diagnosis and treatment."

"That's where he wanted to put you," Jonah mumbles to me a little too loudly, much to Jofra's dismay and embarrassment.

"The safety of our council and our citizens is not a question of personal affiliation or preference, but a responsibility," Jofra continues, barely missing a beat, and quickly changing the subject as we approach a large set of double doors. "We are now about to enter one of the most interesting, and potentially disturbing, areas of the facility. Please be aware that what you see here may not make for pleasant viewing but is fundamental to our understanding of the current Panacean regime, and the information we believe it is unlawfully withholding."

Suddenly, this quaint little guided tour has taken a sinister edge. Even Jonah seems uncomfortable, clearly uncertain himself of what we are about to be shown.

"Anything else, Ally Cohen?"

My grandfather looks steadfastly at each of our party: me, Jonah, Jofra…before finally lingering on Summerhythe.

"As far as I am aware, no one from outside of these walls has ever been shown what you are about to see. Whilst I'm not fully convinced that this is the right decision at this stage, what *is* certain is that we now feel an obligation to make our findings known to a larger audience, especially those who are unwittingly subjecting themselves to such distressing fates."

What on earth are they holding in there?

My eyes wander beyond Jofra's left shoulder to a discreet plaque on the door not far behind him, which reads:

PANACEA VACCINE RESEARCH FACILITY.
AUTHORISED PERSONNEL ONLY.

For a moment, I realise I've stopped breathing and consciously feel the need to draw breath into my lungs. My whole body is suddenly on edge…

Well, we've come this far…?

"No turning back now I suppose," Jonah says, once again stealing my thoughts.

He's getting good at that.

Chapter Twenty-Five

At first glance, it's hardly a horror show.

I don't know what I expected – alarms, thrashing bodies with crazed eyes and panicking doctors desperately trying to sedate them – but the room is still, and quiet, except for the metronomic beep of monitors and the mechanical inhale and release of some sort of respirator. I count nine cubicles, each covered on all sides by heavy duty transparent material – *like giant ice-cubes,* I think, then I quickly refocus.

"Where shall we begin?"

"Eight."

Jofra arches a cautious eyebrow towards my grandfather.

"Eight?"

"We agreed to use the opportunity to progress quickly. We mustn't shy away from the severity of the situation."

Far from convinced, Jofra nevertheless leads us to the far side of the room and stops just short of cubicle 8. Again, he appears to seek assurance from my grandfather, who nods, and silently we pass through a doorway which is unsealed and resealed immediately after our entry. Again, no instant cause for concern: a patient, nearly fully covered in light cotton, face fitted with a respirator which seems to be dictating the rhythm and frequency of breaths. Compared to the council meeting the previous night, this environment appears positively serene, but Jofra's face tells a different story.

"Patient 8. Like all of the patients here in this ward, Patient 8 is Panacean – that is to say, has received the Panacea vaccine. Unlike most Panaceans, before her 60th year, having grown wary of The Panacean Council and the notion of their so-called *Heaven,* Patient 8 sought escape and fled here to The Ether, where she remained in good health, until shortly after her 60th birthday."

Jofra pauses momentarily, giving an opportunity for questioning, but everyone hangs upon his words.

"Shortly thereafter, as we have observed with all similar cases, Patient 8 began to deteriorate at an ever-increasing rate. This appears to manifest itself in instability at a *cellular* level.

"Essentially, once the vaccine's predetermined lifespan has passed, the cells themselves begin to die resulting in necrosis. If you look here, upon the face, you will see areas of relatively mild discolouration and marbling, whereas upon the body there are, well, expansive areas of severe necrosis through autolysis, or self-ingestion."

Summerhythe turns pale.

"Cells are *eating* themselves?"

"In the plainest terms, that may be the shortest route to understanding…yes."

"Then, below…"

We all look to the thin, cotton sheet covering the torso and lower body of Patient 8.

"And they just…?"

"The mortality rate is 100%, yes," Jofra explains, "We are merely giving them the most comfortable end-of-life care that we are able. Of these nine currently surviving Panaceans—"

"Currently?"

"Yes, sadly we have been unable, so far, to reverse any of the deterioration that is occurring."

"How many to date?"

Jofra looks solemn.

"42 patients so far. And I can't deny that I expect that number to rise to 51 within a week."

I look around at the nine patients surrounding us, and the inevitability of it all sends a chill down my spine. Summerhythe steps forward, towards the patient before us.

"I need to see it."

"I would advise on the strongest terms that Cressida and Jonah step outside."

My grandfather looks to me for a decision – he won't dictate on my behalf.

"I'd like to stay," I reply. Jofra, clearly far from convinced, removes the thin veneer of white cotton hesitantly, and unveils a sight I knew immediately that I'd never be able to unsee.

Large areas of flesh are simply devoid of *skin* and, being exposed to the air, have toughened into what appears to be flaking green-black scales of raw tissue. I force my eyes to stay trained upon the sight and appear unmoved, but my brain is telling me to do everything in my power to get as far away as possible. It is unimaginable to think of the discomfort – a life reduced to a shell; a husk, with silver hair, just like…

Images of my grandmother flood my mind. Since her Ascension, I'd so wanted to believe she was walking along those beaches, just like in the film – smiling, amongst friends…somewhere. But where is *Somewhere?* Heaven? If so, where is it, and does it even exist?

Suddenly, my hands are grasping Summerhythe's collar and I'm screaming those same questions directly at her.

"Where is it?!"

"What?"

"Heaven? Where is it? Or have you been lying to us this whole time?"

"No!"

"Then tell me!"

"I don't know —"

"TELL ME!"

My hand is raised now — I want to hurt her.

"Cress!"

Jonah grabs me, and with one swift motion I find myself several feet away from Summerhythe, who now seems to be crying.

"I don't know! I didn't know…" she sobs.

My blood is still racing through my veins, but I still can't help feeling a little sorry for lashing out. I won't cry though. I can't — there'll be time for that later.

"I need to get back to The Panaceum and my mother."

"All in good time," my grandfather says, attempting to quell my rage.

"That's the thing, isn't it? We don't *have* time."

With that, I turn on my heels and storm out of the cubicle, knowing all eyes are now fixed upon me. It doesn't matter…

"I'm going home!" I yell over my shoulder. "And then I'm going to find Heaven."

Chapter Twenty-Six

Jonah stands silhouetted against the blazing backdrop of an Etherian sunset. His pod looks very different in this light and, looking down at the calm waters glimmering below, it's hard to imagine a more peaceful scene. Inside, my guts are churning, anticipating what's ahead. We've agreed to leave at first light, giving us the best chance of making the journey in a single day. I repack my bag, carefully placing the new medications alongside the LAI gun and other items. There is a knock at the door. Jonah answers, and I am surprised to see him return with my grandfather.

"I was hoping we might talk."

Jonah needs no further encouragement and nods, before promptly leaving.

For the first time, I stand alone – face-to-face – with my grandfather, but strangely I have no urge to be sentimental. This whole thing is now so much bigger than either of us.

"How long have you known?" I venture.

"Known…?"

"That The Panacea *does* that to people."

The air hangs heavy as if my grandfather already knows where this is heading.

"We've always suspected that there must be some side-effect, some sort of consequence from such a drastic vaccine, and times were so desperate that it was barely tested. Only in the past few years have we had the proof —"

"A few years?" I interrupt "Then how *could* you?"

"How could I what?"

"Let her go to Heaven!"

He looks at me. My tone was sharper, angrier than I intended, but it didn't make the question any less valid...or the answer any less surprising.

"Let her?" he smiles, as he walks over and perches himself on the edge of the bed, looking out over his world: "She insisted; it was her idea."

He exhales, long and low and hurting, and suddenly the 'Sovereign of The Ether' is nothing more than an aging man before me, pining for the love of his life. I join him, looking out into and abyss of burning sky and water, and say nothing. Seconds, maybe minutes, pass – it doesn't seem to matter. Words come eventually.

"Our families were on separate sides of the issue – your grandmother's and mine. We were too young to have a choice; she was vaccinated, I wasn't. It really didn't seem to mean much to begin with. Then, in what seemed like no time at all, my family and I were being forced to leave, alongside many of the families who had helped establish The Panaceum."

"And my grandmother?"

"She followed. Gave up the security of The Panaceum for a dangerous wilderness with no guarantee of safety. The road wasn't easy for us – we lost...many."

The weight of the memory is visible is his face – bitterness still raw, almost palpable.

"And now you want your home back?"

"Now we have no choice. We found refuge here in The Ether and adapted to this world above the water. We established a means of keeping ourselves safe and gained advantage over many of the clusters who roam outside of The Panaceum. But…"

He rises and edges forward towards the window-wall before us, as I wonder exactly what he means by *clusters*.

"Time is running out," he continues. "Water levels are rising still further and the structures you see around you, once great landmarks within the city of London, weren't built to withstand the pressures that they are under now."

I think back to the previous evening's metallic groans from the deep. It never really occurred to me that the very foundations that The Ether stood upon might be giving way beneath us.

"We needed a plan: Operation Providence."

"Ezra told me: infiltrate Panacean society, integrate until it was impossible to decipher who was who and then live happily ever after."

"Yes, sort of." My grandfather grins. "Years passed. We successfully smuggled tens of Etherian adults back into The Panaceum without issue, but we needed to up the anti: a child born *within* The Panaceum itself would blur the lines between our societies, so much so, that there would be no going back. And that was when she fell pregnant."

"Who?"

"Your mother."

"My mother? But she always seemed, so…"

"Sometimes, we must assume a different attitude to protect those we love. Don't be deceived: your mother is a warrior. As soon as she found out she was with child she insisted on making the journey back to The Panaceum along with your father."

"My father?"

"Yes, he plays a vital role in this story."

I let the words sink in. A side to a woman I'd never seen, and a man I barely knew, but most strikingly...

I was the first Etherian born inside The Panaceum.

"Of course, exposing the ideology of The Panaceum as a sham was only half of the battle. In order to complete the mission, we needed an insight into *Heaven*. Such is the secrecy over Heaven, we were unable to unearth any information as to its location, let alone the conditions and secrets that it may be hiding. As unvaccinated Etherians, there was no chance at all of gaining access via regular means, however it became apparent that there was one among us who may have a...unique opportunity."

"My grandmother."

"Yes. Panaceum born, and vaccinated, she was entitled to her place. She returned to The Panaceum, remorseful for her decision to flee. She was able to obtain a hub and a role within society. Althea would follow on later. By now, we had Etherians in high-ranking positions within The Panaceum. Your mother was given false papers and, after a home birth, you were registered onto the system and, to all intents and purposes, are indeed Panacean."

"Except for the vaccine."

"Yes...that was Ezra's handiwork."

My grandfather refocuses.

"Ida planned to get evidence from Heaven back to the Ether. There was talk of concealing a recording device, of damning videos being beamed, but…"

Tears now well in my grandfather's eyes.

"So far, we've had nothing. I told her – I said it was far too dangerous, that there were no guarantees, but Ida, she was –"

"A warrior," I interject.

"Yes. And an activist. And a truth-seeker. And she would be so, so proud of you, my dear."

Chapter Twenty-Seven

I wake with a start. Jonah stands in his usual spot, peering out over a star-spangled night through binoculars. I wonder whether he ever sleeps. He's looking down to the water, and as I sit up slowly, I notice tension in his posture. Come to think of it, I didn't simply wake at all...I was woken.

I hear light scuttering sounds against metalwork: I want to believe it's rain or hail, but the skies are clear, and Jonah now frantically crosses the pod, obviously searching out the source of the sound.

"Jonah?"

"Get your stuff."

I don't question it.

I'm still wearing the neoprene suit I've been given. Yes, it's uncomfortable, but Jonah described it as a second skin, and I'm thankful for it now as I grab my bag and make my way to him within a matter of seconds. Whatever is making the sound, it's closer, and my panicked eyes can't avoid posing the obvious question.

"Electromagnets," Jonah responds, which only heightens my confusion, "They're climbing."

"Who?"

"Pirates."

I definitely hear the word, but it seems to send my brain spinning, and I freeze on the spot.

"They're still below," Jonah continues. "Cressida... Cress! I need you to go to the viewing platform and see if there's any way down. Now!"

My legs spring to action, although I'm still caught in a haze.

Outside on the viewing platform, I look down and, sure enough, two figures are scaling the vertical faces of the wheel's metallic rim as easily as if they are scrambling up a gigantic cargo net. At second glance, wires from their wrists and ankles appear to be connected to large packs on their backs, as somehow, they eat up the gap between themselves and me with ease. That same scuttering sound of metal against metal and an echo on Jonah's voice in my mind...

Magnets.

I turn on my heels and sprint back to Jonah, who now stands with a pack upon his own back atop of his bed.

"No way down. They're nearly here."

"Thought not," Jonah says, unmoved. "Up it is then."

With that, he reaches above his head and releases a metal hatch in the roof of the pod and immediately climbs through. A hand appears back through the portal: my invitation to follow. I look to the security screen by the side of the door to see two figures emerge over the brim of the platform outside.

Up it is.

I clamber onto the bed, and grab the outstretched hand presented to me.

"Ready?"

My legs are coiled, ready to spring upward but, as I do, a glaring flash blinds me as my whole body is thrown from the bed onto the ground below.

An explosion.

Pain surges through my hip as I desperately attempt to regain my footing. Jonah's hand is no longer at the portal. My eyes search frantically around the room. The door to the pod is simply a wall of electrical fire now, which quickly subsides, and two frenetic figures dash through and lock eyes with mine, widening.

Am I...their target?

No time.

"Cress!"

Jonah is back at the portal.

The pirates launch themselves towards me as I lunge and grab Jonah's hand, which almost pulls my arm out of its socket as it yanks me up, and out into the night air.

The hatch slams shut behind us.

It's a mild night, yet the wind still howls high above the water, and I struggle to understand how we're any better off out here than we would be in there. Jonah's hand is raised above his head, and he seems to be assessing...the air?

"What are you doing?" I demand.

Behind me, I can hear the pirates. Judging by the light work they made of the pod door, the hatch won't hold for long.

"Do you trust me?" Jonah calls, offering me his outstretched hand.

"What?"

"Do you trust me?"

I don't know where this is heading, but I know the answer. "Yes."

Another explosion, and I just know the hatch has gone and the pirates are upon us. None of that matters though as Jonah has pulled me tight into him and, without warning, thrown us into an abyss from the top of one of the tallest structures in London.

We're falling. No, not falling, hurtling through the air, the sound of the wind almost deafening as I cling to Jonah, head buried in his chest. My heart pounds as though it wants to leave my body, but my curiosity burns, and I turn my head to try and catch a glimpse of what on Earth is happening. Jonah's face is being beaten furiously by the oncoming air, but his steely eyes are unflinching. He moves a hand towards his backpack, and a cord I hadn't noticed before. Suddenly, a wave of relief engulfs me as I imagine the possibility of a parachute, or – *zwoosh!*

I don't know what else I'd been expecting but it wasn't wings.

A huge swathe of enveloped material begins to unfurl at either side of Jonah's back, reaching into the sky, propelling us out and away from the pirates on the currents of the air above the surrounding waters. With all the exhilaration, I've dug my nails into his lower back, and I release my grip a little as Jonah takes hold of two controls which appear to manipulate the wings.

We soar and surge though the Ether air with ease; Jonah skilfully negotiating the currents and the network of tall buildings and elevated walkways. With the prospect of imminent death behind us (for now), I dare to take in more of my surroundings. I needn't have bothered; at this speed everything is a mass blur, which makes Jonah's precision all the more impressive. He calls from above.

"We're approaching The Shard!"

I crane my neck, and up ahead a can see the council building looming.

"Brace yourself – I've never carried someone before, let alone try to land with them!"

"Oh great!" I holler back, but still, I know for certain I'd rather be taking my chances here than back there with the pirates.

All at once, Jonah pulls hard on the wing's controls sending them flipping, at odds with the direction of travel, instantly killing our momentum as we approach landing. I'm not exactly sure what 'bracing myself' is meant to entail, but instinctively I tense and hold on tighter. My eyes close as Jonah's feet pound the floor beneath us, but instantly we're airborne again, then feet again, then a tumble which sends us spinning until, eventually, we come to a stop.

I can feel Jonah beneath me, his chest beating against my own as I wait for him to open his eyes. He appears to have taken the brunt of the fall, twisting so the pack upon his back provided a cushion between us and the ground below. Still, it had been heavy.

Seconds pass before Jonah opens his eyes.

"Are you okay?" he whispers.

"Yes, are you?"

"I'll live," he says with a grin.

And then something in his eye changes, to which mine instantly responds, and with his breath upon my face I feel an overwhelming urge to move my lips closer to his. Somewhere, the pirates are planning their next move, but none of that matters right here and now. My eyes begin to close gently as my mouth slowly approaches his.

And then I stop, abruptly.

24–48 hours…

Jofra's voice: there's still a chance I could by harbouring diphtheria.

I want to explain this to Jonah, but before I have the chance, hurried footsteps approach.

"What happened?" Jofra yells, closely followed by Summerhythe and my grandfather.

"Pirates! They must have known…"

"Known what?"

"That Cressida was with me."

So I *was* the target.

"Why me?" I question.

"You're the granddaughter of the Sovereign. You're…valuable."

"But how *could* they know?" my grandfather demands.

"That's exactly what I'd like to find out."

"There's no time," Jofra interjects, "this is a unique opportunity for the pirates, they're not going to give up easily. We need to get Cressida back to The Panaceum immediately."

"Right. The quickest way would be to take the jet-ski," Jonah insists, making his way to the landing bay. "The waters are calm. Yes, it'll be cold, but if Cressida and I set off now we can make it…"

"I think I should come too."

It's Summerhythe. All eyes turn upon her, but Jonah is quick to dismiss the idea.

"No chance. The jet-ski holds two at a push, and we can't tow the dinghy, we'll be too slow – these guys *live* on the water, they'll eat up the gap in no time at all."

"Then I should go *instead,*" Summerhythe insists, to Jonah's clear dismay. Still, she continues, "I need to do this. And I'm Cressida's best chance of getting back into The Panaceum without raising alarm or undue suspicion. With my I.D., I can take her straight through the front door: no Harvesters, no sewers, no unknowns. Then we can get straight to the task of treating your mother and exposing The Panaceum's lies. Some of these wrongs are my fault: I want to be part of putting them right. I owe you this."

Jonah motions as if to tear her down before seeming to realise that he's in the presence of two elders. He looks to Jofra who, in turn, looks to my grandfather for a decision.

And my grandfather, once again, looks to me.

"She's right," I offer cautiously.

In the distance, a bell sounds.

"Someone must have spotted the pirates, or more are approaching. If they think the game's up, they may just mount a full-on attack." Jonah explains.

"In that case, it makes even more sense. Stay here, defend the Ether, and follow on if a safe opportunity arises."

The authoritative tone in my voice surprises even me, but instinctively I have already taken the LAI Gun out of my bag and am making my way to the jet-ski before anyone has the chance to intervene. A quick tour of the basic controls and I'm thankful for the sleeked-oil stillness of the sea before me.

Saddled on the jet-ski with Summerhythe close behind, I reach out and squeeze Jonah's hand, hard.

"Thank you. For the harvester, returning me, saving me…thank you."

He smiles sheepishly, completely at odds with the heroism that seems to come to him so naturally.

"Here," he says, "take this with you."

He removes a necklace and carefully places it around my neck. A set of wings: angels wings which fall either side of a blue sphere.

"Thank you."

I channel Jonah now as I make final mental checks and brace myself for the crossing.

"I'll see you all soon!" I shout, as the engine comes to life and with a sharp twist of the throttle-grip we speed off, blindly, across the Oxford Strait.

Chapter Twenty-Eight

Looking back at The Ether from the shoreline in the morning sun, there's no sign of the night's conflict. My bones ache. *Sleep* has been nothing more than a series of uncomfortable fits and starts: for me, at least – Summerhythe is still dozing nearby. Our journey back across the water had been a silent one, as had the process of concealing the jet-ski with shrubbery and finding a place to rest our heads for the night.

I will the life back into my legs and wander along the shoreline: after all, who knows when I'll be back here – if I'll be back here. I could never have imagined this world a few days ago: vast expanses of open space and water, vaulting skies, sprawling woodlands where the trees and shrubs have not been laid out in neat rows, pruned and precise. A breeze brushes past me fuelled with the smell of salt water and fresh air. I feel at home here. Connected. Not that I'd *not* felt at home in The Panaceum; until now, I'd just never had any reason to doubt it.

I find myself wondering if the similar is true for Summerhythe. If she'd been fed the same stories as I had – been shown the same videos of plagues, and vaccines, and Heaven – then why would she have reason to suspect that there's anything different?

Footsteps approach and it's Summerhythe herself, looking weary and uncomfortable in both her neoprene and the wild surroundings.

"Morning."

"Morning."

It's our first tentative step towards a conversation since leaving the Ether. She stops walking and I feel obliged to do the same.

"I wanted to tell you that I'm sorry," Summerhythe begins, "I feel...naïve. But I was born Panacean: I went straight from being educated by the system, to educating on behalf of the system. I haven't known anything else, and I've always been so willing to take whatever they said at face value. Why wouldn't I? But now...now, I can't even begin to..."

"It's okay," I interrupt, sensing that if I don't, she is going to break down and, let's face it, before all this she was my schoolteacher so that would just be...awkward. "Until recently, I'd barely questioned it either."

"Thank you," Summerhythe says, looking relieved.

As we begin our trek back to The Panaceum, we discuss our approach, and hope that keeping the sun at our backs will be enough to maintain or course due west. If not, we'd have to follow our noses and, luckily, The Panaceum can be seen from many miles around.

It doesn't take long before Summerhythe and I are chatting about Panacean life. It turns out that she lives alone in Citi-bloc 9 and describes how balancing life as a teacher and a council operative isn't always easy. I mention school and the 'perfect heal' in her Art Class.

"I remember that day!" Summerhythe chimes, "You looked so bewildered, then so —"

"Uncomfortable?"

"I was going to say *happy.*"

Despite myself, I'm laughing. We're both laughing. But that's where it ends: I don't mention anything more about perfect heals, tattoos or otherwise. I'm unsure how much she knows — or doesn't know — about any of those things, and I'm certainly not planning to be the person who fills in any gaps.

"I hope you know that when I came to your house that day, I was only doing my job. Just like when I tracked you out here, I thought I was protecting my home, my family, and now I see —"

"I know," I say. Again, I feel bad for interjecting but all of that seems so unimportant now. I step up another gear and we push on through heat of the early afternoon.

By mid-afternoon, after a period of thinking we'd veered off course, The Panaceum thankfully appears on the horizon, and by dusk, we are only a few hundred metres from an imposing boundary control checkpoint: the gateway between The Panaceum and the wilderness.

I'm now walking ahead of Summerhythe with an improvised strapping 'securing' my hands behind my back. The plan is simple: act as though Summerhythe's mission was successful. She's tracked me down and is simply returning an escapee to The Panacean Council authorities. She's now wearing my backpack, which I'm not thrilled about but finishes the illusion, and I've concealed the LAI gun within my hand strapping as an insurance. It's not perfect, but right now it seems a lot better than trudging through 10 miles of sewer tunnels.

As we're about to make the approach, I hear a light sob behind me.

"Sorry," Summerhythe whimpers. "Being back here...makes it all so real. I've been stupid and —" A bigger sob now. "I have family...in Heaven."

"I think we all do," I offer, "but the only chance they have of finding out what's going on there, is by buckling up and getting on with it."

"You're right."

With that, Summerhythe applies a hand to my shoulder and guides me (gently) towards the checkpoint. Guards stand, heavily armed, though we don't break stride as we pass the outer security with absolute assurance. At the first physical barrier we stop at a booth where a dour-looking attendant gives no indication at all of how to proceed.

"Chief PCO Clarice Summerhythe, working under the authority of UCL-544, Operation Code: 'KLEPTO'."

Without prompting, Summerhythe places her finger on a nearby scanner, which obviously brings various details up onto a monitor within the booth, and the attendant now reads. As I stand surrounded by guards with Summerhythe at my back, it's the first time I've felt like it would be so simple for Summerhythe to just hand me over. Here. Now.

My stomach churns slightly as I consider the possibility that at the very first hurdle, I've walked into a trap. I think of Jonah risking his life; my grandfather, Mother, Ezra, all counting on me...then my grandmother. I feel sick as my hands grip the LAI gun at my back. Slowly, my finger hovers over the trigger. I could swivel and hit Summerhythe's neck easily, but what would that achieve? Far better to take her hostage and negotiate an escape. I'd seen what the LAI gun had done to Jonah's leg, at Summerhythe's temple I'm sure they'd take me seriously.

My mouth is now completely dry as I study the face of the attendant. Any sign of suspicion and I make my move: if this is a trap, I won't be going down without putting up a...

"I'll need a vehicle too. Don't worry about a driver."

I turn to Summerhythe who, with a glint in her eye, gives an almost imperceptible nod of assurance. I attempt to return a nod that says *I wasn't about to anesthetise you, honest,* and loosen my grip on the LAI gun, thankful for my restraint.

Without further ado, the seemingly satisfied attendant passes a black fob through a small opening in the window, which Summerhythe grabs.

"Round the side: vehicle code is on the fob."

"Thanks," she replies and, with a firm push between my shoulder blades – for effect – we head off in the direction of some black people-carriers beyond the barriers.

We're back on Panacean soil.

Sitting in the car, Summerhythe sighs gently.

"See, straight through. I told you."

I smile but decide not to mention my bout of uneasiness.

"Now," she continues with renewed determination, "Where are we heading?"

Chapter Twenty-Nine

Citi-bloc 7. Home. This lift.

Here we are again: racing at high speed towards Ezra's hub and, with any luck, my mother's rescue – if we're not already too late. This time round, I'm with Summerhythe and something feels…different. My eyes scan the same old chrome walls, the control panel, the separate panel with the glowing 'A' for the Ascension Deck…

I wonder how many people have pushed that button in the hope – the *expectation* – of taking their rightful place in Heaven with all that it offered. And where are they now? What's become of them? I find myself physically shaking the thought from my head as it sends a shudder through me. I can't think about that now. All my attention turns to saving my mother, but as the lift *pings* to announce our arrival at our chosen floor, the doors part, and any of the resolve I'd managed to restore immediately drains away from me.

BE VIGILANT:
ANTI-VAXXERS MAY HARBOUR UNKNOWN
VIRUSES FROM BEYOND THE PANACEUM.

The poster is the height of the entire wall before us; the letters themselves nearly as large as I am – dark, heavy font. No graphics. No gimmicks. Just a stark warning signed off by The Panacean Council.

"Come on," Summerhythe urges, but even she seems unsettled by such an open display of caution. Not even a hint of subtlety: they were clearly anxious – and that would make our task all the more difficult.

I continue left out of the lift, and again from the lobby, uneasy strides gathering pace as the sinking feeling in my guts grows. I want to dismiss it, I want to believe that I'm just over-reacting, but as I round the corner it becomes clear my instincts were right.

Ezra's door is sealed with black and yellow tape; on it, a white notice. I could have guessed what it was going to say before I even read it.

ENTRY TO THIS PROPERTY IS STRICTLY
PROHIBITED
UNDER THE ONGOING KLEPTO INITIATIVE
BY ORDER OF THE PANACEAN COUNCIL

"What does it mean?" I demand, wheeling round to Summerhythe who stands at my shoulder.

"Well, it means the property is probably being investigated for –"

"*Klepto*! You used it at the boundary checkpoint too. What does it mean?"

"Well, in the simplest terms," Summerhythe begins, clearly choosing her words more carefully now, "It means 'to steal'. In this case, The Panaceum."

"Steal? But how can they steal what was already theirs?"

"I know the stories, but The Panacean Council believes that they made a choice. This is the safest and most stable place on Earth…it stands to reason that it would be sought-after by those on the outside. Paranoia is rife."

"But they don't want to steal it, they want to *share* it."

"That's not a risk the council is prepared to take."

"Risk? But the vaccine…"

Even as I say the words I stop, as I notice Summerhythe nodding, ruefully. She inches closer, whispering low and steady as she attempts to convey an exterior calm.

"Viruses mutate, Cressida. I shouldn't be saying this to you, especially not here, but in reality, there is no way to know whether the Panacea vaccine is absolutely infallible. We've never needed to worry because we have managed to lock down our boundaries entirely, but anyone incoming could – potentially – be a carrier of something unprecedented. It's not something we shout about…but it's something the council takes deadly seriously."

The inflection of the final few words leaves little room for doubt: I'm a threat…and this is life or death.

Despite knowing that there is no chance they are still inside, I need to see for myself. It sounds silly, but it's the last place that I saw them. Without thinking, I'm peeling back strips of black and yellow tape from the doorframe.

"What are you doing?"

"I'm going in," I reply, stepping back and bracing myself to throw a foot, my whole body, whatever it takes at the door.

"Cressida…"

"You can't stop me!"

"Cressida…"

"I need to do this!"

"Cressida, LISTEN!" Summerhythe blares, "I don't know who you think you are, or what you think that door is made from but...I have an override code for the lock so just...calm down. Please."

Pride slightly dented, I step aside, allowing Summerhythe to navigate the lock system and gain access. Inside, lies darkness.

"Intellihub, L-5. Confirm."

As the light rises, tears begin.

A life in pieces. The main living space is completely trashed, but that holds little interest as I run towards the second bedroom: the table where the sewer map lay is overturned, discarded towels lie around the chair where I last saw my mother, but most strikingly, the books...the books have gone.

I feel the energy drain away from me, tempting me to buckle at the knees but, unlike the Cressida who left The Panaceum, the tears I shed are not of despair, but anger. They burn my cheeks.

"Where now?"

"Cressida, I'm sorry —"

"Where?"

Summerhythe needs no further explanation.

"Well, they can only be at The Panacean Council building. A breach like this would go directly to the top, to Roman."

"Roman?"

"Chief of The Panacean Council; leader of Operation Klepto. He pulls the strings."

"Then why are we still here?"

Summerhythe ambles towards the centre of the room and sighs as she slowly takes in the destruction. I persevere.

"What's wrong?"

"Getting you back into The Panaceum was one thing – that's just the cage. *This* would mean heading into the mouth of the lion. It's dangerous, and they don't take kindly to unexpected visitors."

She looks to her wrist.

"Damn. They took my comms unit back at the Ether, I have no way of calling ahead. There's a service phone back in the lobby. I'll meet you by the lift."

"Well, I'll just come with you –"

"I need you to stay and search the place…depending on how this goes, we might need a weapon. See what you can find."

With that, she leaves and I begin scrambling around unsure of what kind of weapon would give us any chance against The Panacean Council. Where would I even begin to look in a place that has already been scoured.

My eyes dart to the map of the United Kingdom, which still hangs on the far wall, seemingly untouched. I peel it back to reveal the recess where Ezra had originally produced the LAI gun from days earlier. It's hardly the arsenal of weaponry I was hoping for but, in the circumstances, it would have to do. There's a small switchblade knife, which I immediately tuck under the ankle of my neoprene suit, before removing a small bottle which rattles around in my hand. The label makes for grim reading.

'LAST RESORT'

I open the bottle to find a small capsule, which I can only assume must be some sort of suicide pill. It's hardly the beacon of hope I was looking for. That said, if I was cornered and interrogated, I find myself thinking that using it would be better than ruining the decades of risk and preparation involved in Operation Providence and the plight of my people.

My people.

The words linger in my head, renewing my sense of purpose, and as I put the bottle in my pack I feel a strange sense of assurance that my destiny is ultimately in my own hands. There's one final item in the recess: a ring, with a large, black stone. On closer inspection, however, it's not actually a stone at all, but a glass casing of some sort. Like the bottle, it too has instructions in small lettering on its base.

1. SHIELD EYES
2. BREAK GLASS
3. RUN

I have no indication of what to expect from the ring, but I find that it fits (albeit loosely) on the middle finger of my right hand. And with that, the recess is empty and I flee towards the lift, where Summerhythe is waiting.

"Find something?"

"Yes, a switchblade and –"

"Good," Summerhythe interrupts, "we need to be quick, apparently the interrogation has started…and your mother is weakening. They're expecting us. Same drill: I'm returning an escapee. Once we get there, I'll get you into a holding cell with your mother and Ezra and smuggle in the medication."

"And then?"

"Well, then…I'm still working on it. But we'll need to get creative. Now, come on."

Chapter Thirty

The mouth of the lion.

Gloucester Cathedral has stood here since the eleventh century, although significant restorations have taken place since that time, both inside and out. Notable features include Gothic architecture and the soaring stained-glass features of the West Window, as well as the famous four pinnacles that adorn its central tower.

Apparently, those History classes did come in handy after all. That said, although I seem to have talked about it endlessly, I've never stood as close as I am now, having bypassed the perimeter security. Nothing could have prepared me for its old-world majesty and grandeur. After all, this is it, Ground Zero: the place where the very first Panaceans found sanctuary and dared to dream of a life beyond the destruction of the New Plague. These days, citi-blocs and skyscrapers dwarf this site, but there is undoubtedly nowhere more sacred in all of The Panaceum.

"Impressive, isn't it?" Summerhythe says through a smile.

"Yes. It's a shame it's come to this."

"It is, yes. It's always been such a peaceful place."

"Well, we're not here for a war: we're here for answers, and justice."

"Quite right. Are you ready?"

"Yes," I reply – and I am, though Summerhythe has a final few instructions before move ahead.

"Once we get inside, leave the talking to me. Obviously, we need to maintain the pretence of me returning an escapee. But don't worry, they won't arrest you: you're fifteen-years-old and, as far as they're concerned, you were coerced into a plan you knew little-to-nothing about."

I nod, reassured – glad for once that they *wouldn't* be treating me like an adult.

"A few things will happen once we get inside," she continues. "Security is tight, so they'll want your bag. Don't worry though, I'll get that back to you once we're in a position to deliver and administer the medication to your mother and Ezra. They may also take your prints for their database. Again, this is just procedure. Ready?"

I nod for a final time, and we begin walking. With every step I take, I think of the Panaceans who have walked them before me, and the Etherians who will walk them in the future.

We're close now.

If I thought I felt small standing outside the building, then I feel twice as small now looking up at the vast, vaulted ceiling, towering above me. I am stood in the beating heart of The Panaceum, ready to stand against what, until recently, I'd believed was perfect system. Looking around, the achievement is undoubtedly monumental…but it was not reached alone. I tune in to Summerhythe who, again, has taken the lead and speaks to one of the many uniformed personnel.

"Yes. CPCO Payton should be expecting us…"

Everyone around us seems occupied – patrolling or talking into headsets – and I wonder what they could be expecting that would warrant the number of armed guards who are encamped in the foyer.

"Agent Summerhythe."

Unlike the uniformed officers around us, the suited man approaching was not obviously armed which, surprisingly, seemed only to highlight his authority. He was tall, and completely bald creating the impression of a streamlined and hardened exterior. That said, his voice is deep and gentle – almost artificially so – as he continues.

"I'm glad to see you made it back safely. I had my doubts, especially when I heard of the pursuit through that sewer."

Now he looks to me, and smiles. Again, it's unnervingly gentle, as though he almost appreciates the lengths I have gone to.

"Ingenious really. I expect the Ether was quite an eye-opener for you both."

"It's good to be back, sir. Glad to have done my duty."

"And done it well," Payton continues before diverting his attention back to me. "The other two captives have, thus far, proved rather stubborn, let's hope that you choose to be more pragmatic, especially given their delicate situation."

I can't help myself.

"Where are they? I need to…"

Payton raises his right hand in the air – but that alone is not the reason I stop talking.

Every single armed officer is now training their gun on *me*.

You won't be arrested.

Frantically, my eyes search for Summerhythe, but when my gaze meets hers all she offers is a steely glare before diverting her attention to the ground by her feet.

That's what she said.

Payton is now behind me removing my backpack – and with it, the medications for my mother and Ezra.
You won't be arrested.
"Cressida Conners, you are hereby being held under suspicion of conspiring against The Panaceum. Take her to the cloisters, so we may begin questioning."
As he speaks the words, restraints are being placed firmly around my wrists and I am forcibly being led from the scene.

You won't be arrested, she'd said!

"Sir!" Summerhythe interrupts.
And suddenly, it's okay, it's all part of the plan. I steal a glance over my shoulder and, in that moment, a searing pain rips through me, and my hope dies.

No...

"You may wish to search about her person," Summerhythe says, "I have reason to believe she is carrying a blade."

...we're not on the same team.

Chapter Thirty-One

"Summerhythe!" I scream, until I feel bile rise in the back of my throat. Not that I care: I've never been so angry. "Summerhythe! I know you're watching!"

I glare at the surveillance unit in the corner of the room above the door. I've been led along what used to be cloisters in the Cathedral – huge stained-glass windows adorning the walls, vaulted ceilings with sprawling, intricate patterns carved from stone. The room I'm being held in is far from the grandeur of outside: four walls, a table and two chairs – of which, all the moveable items are firmly fixed to the floor.

Yes, I've checked.

Even so, I kick out again at one of the chairs. Useless, but I need to vent, I *need* to get their attention somehow. Stomping and screaming have so far failed and, I'm not sure why yet, but I find myself approaching the door, fuelled by instinct and adrenaline. I jump and claw at the surveillance – it's within reach, but I'm not really hopeful of carrying out much damage. I try again with little effect. Rage still coursing through my veins, I tear off one of my shoes and begin braying the unit again and again as I continue to scream, fully aware that I must look possessed.

"Summerhythe!"

"Sit down please, Miss Conners."

A male voice from the security unit.

"No! I'm not doing a thing until she looks me in the eye and tells me *why!*"

I hurl my boot at the unit, again doing little damage, but the physical release is welcome.

"Miss Conners, please –"

"No!"

I'm climbing up onto the table now.

"You're a coward! Jonah wanted to kill you from the off, and I convinced him not to…and this is how you repay me? Come in here and face me! What's the matter? Can't bear to –"

"Sit down, Cressida."

Her voice is measured, and sounds tinny through the speaker, but it's Summerhythe. I want to keep screaming and shouting, but the rage suddenly gets overtaken by a sense of deep betrayal that seems to start crushing me within.

"How…could you?"

"The risk, Cressida: the risk is just too great. Everything you see, everything we've achieved took huge sacrifice."

"And what about the Etherians? What about their sacrifice? And what about the vaccine and its side-effects, and Heaven? You said yourself, you have people there…what about *them*?"

The static buzz of an open line lingers for a number of seconds, until words finally come.

"That's the system we signed up to. That's the deal we make."

"But it's *not!* You saw those people – those bodies – it's a lie! And what…what about my mother? You let me get all the way back here, clinging onto those medications for dear life. Please…"

"I'm sorry, Cressida."

"No! You can't do that – give her the medication."

The static buzz cuts out as the line goes dead.

"Summerhythe, give her the medication! I swear to you, if it's the last thing I do, I will hunt you down and…"

Suddenly, the electronic lock on the door springs into life. It appears to have been released. I lower myself from the table into one of the chairs below and wait to see who appears.

Voices come into range: an older, authoritative male voice mutters words I can't really make out, followed by Summerhythe.

"I just don't think it's wise."

"I understand your concern," the authoritative voice continues, "but she's a minor, and I think we can afford to try and establish some level of trust considering she's hardly a ring-leader in this operation."

No response comes, as the door begins to open slowly.

I shift in my seat as a tall, straight, figure appears in the doorway. Immediately, I'm drawn to a set of grey eyes that look both striking and lost all at once. They gaze at me, full of curiosity and, I sense, wonderment as if I'm an oddity, almost, like something from a museum.

"I've been waiting a long time to meet you in the flesh."

"Yes, well, I didn't have much choice in the matter," I scoff.

I see the corner of his mouth curl ever so slightly as he makes his way to the chair opposite me and sits, never once averting his gaze.

"My name is Roman. I thought we might talk for a few moments – just you and me."

With that, he raises his hand and immediately the light on the surveillance unit fades to black.

"I can assure you, we're now alone. I often find the thought of prying eyes and ears can be off-putting when you're simply trying to have a conversation."

I avert my gaze in case he notices any softening in my demeanour.

"Cressida," he continues, "I need you to tell me everything you know about Operation Providence."

Any softening within me quickly disappears.

"Withholding information could have serious consequences...and not just for you Cressida."

Slowly, he removes two vials from his pocket and places them on the table between us.

"I know how much your mother and Ezra mean to you."

I stare at the medication on the table, fighting back the surge of desperation to reach out and grab them.

I got so close. So close.

"All that I'm asking, is that you consider what is in the best interests of your family and tell me what you know."

I think about everything I could lose: my future, my family, my life. Then I think about the family that I've gained, The Ether, and what they'd all given up to get to this point. It was enough for my mother and grandmother to live for decades in secrecy: important enough that Ezra was willing to risk his own life, enough that my family were prepared to live half of their lifetimes hundreds of miles apart. So important that, even now, my grandmother was in Heaven attempting to expose a corrupt system, possibly undergoing immeasurable suffering herself…

"I won't do it."

"Not even to save your own mother?"

"But I am…I'm saving what she's fought all her life for."

There is no doubt in my voice.

Roman nods steadily and rises, making his way towards the door.

"You know," he says, turning, "you remind me a lot of her."

I remain seated, baffled.

"Follow me," he continues, before looking down at the medications which he has left upon the table.

"And bring those with you."

Chapter Thirty-Two

We've taken a sharp left out of the room I was being held in and zig-zagged through a maze of corridors, each further and further from the modern image of the council building displayed in the foyer. It is even more obvious now as we descend a set of large, stone steps that spiral down into the bowels of the cathedral. The air has changed – dank, musty – and the temperature drops immediately as we continue further into the building's original foundations.

No words have been exchanged so far. Roman's strides are brisk and purposeful, but there is no sense of panic even though something seems highly irregular about this whole situation. Not that I mind; I have the medications tight within my grasp, and I have no doubt that this is a significant improvement from being trapped alone in the interrogation room. There's very little light now, and the ground underfoot is broken and uneven. My curiosity gets the better of me.

"Where are we?"

"The crypt," Roman replies without breaking his focus or stride, "Once we get there, we won't have much time."

I feel my heartrate increase at this first definite sign of hope.

"I know this must all seem confusing, but first thing's first – there'll be time for explanations later. Cressida…"

He finally stops. We're standing before a heavy, metallic door that looks alien in these ancient surroundings. Roman aligns his face to a sensor which immediately releases a locking mechanism within.

"…I have to warn you that your mother's condition has deteriorated significantly. There's also little doubt in my mind that Ezra is showing signs of weakness. Don't be afraid – we have the medications. Simply administer them as instructed; let's do this one step at a time."

Tentatively, I cross the threshold and through the gloom I notice a platform against the back wall. Basic sheeting suggests this is a bed of sorts, at either end of which, Ezra and my mother lie unconscious or asleep and the air hums with the nauseating wheezing of their lungs struggling for air. Naturally, I gravitate to my mother and despite my best intentions to keep a level head, a biting shock stops me dead in my tracks as I realise how badly she's deteriorated. Her throat is swollen and throbbing, exaggerated by a feverish redness and visible streaks of sweat cascading from her brow. Despite that, the rest of her body looks gaunt as the woman I knew appears to be fading away before me. I try to shake off the paralysis gripping me, but a small child who never understood her mother's plight and the things she had to sacrifice on her behalf is still there, inside me, and she's frightened. She's petrified at the thought that she's only just realised that this woman before her is her hero, and she might never get the chance to tell her.

I look to Roman, who stands distracted, keeping lookout by the door, and once again, I realise that this whole thing is bigger than Cressida Connors, bigger than my feelings, and the sacrifices of so many are squarely in my hands.

I rip open the first medication pack and, to my surprise, three separate elements fall onto the ground below.

"Damn!" I yell, as a I scramble around feeling foolish.

Thankfully, the plunger, the needle and the anti-toxin itself appear undamaged. Hands shaking, I attach the needle to the plunger and draw the antitoxin from the small, sealed vial as instructed. I use the sheeting to wipe down a spot on my mother's arm, and before I have any further chance to think about what I'm actually doing, I jab the needle firmly into my mother's bicep and plunge. I don't want to have to do this twice.

I'm not sure what I expected, but my mother remains unmoving, her body still working extremely hard to keep her alive. No quick miracles here.

"Cressida?"

It's Ezra, his voice a shadow of the sagely advisor I'd left only a few days ago. His features too look sallow, and the intricate designs adorning his skin look parched and withered.

"You made it…"

"Just," I reply, readying the second syringe, "it's a long story."

I inject Ezra and, again, there's no instant change, though he raises a relieved smile which further contorts the array of lines and patterns on his face. He drags himself into an upright sitting position and places a hand on my shoulder.

"Thank you."

"Yes, well, I nearly didn't make it. You have Roman to thank for that."

Ezra raises his eyes and, for the first time, notices that Roman is still dutifully on guard by the door. Then, to my surprise, I see tears forming in Ezra's eyes, as he whispers, "I told him. I told him this day would come."

I look to Roman, who also seems to have glassy eyes, then back to Ezra – tears now streaming.

"None of this makes any sense."

In the circumstances, I try not to sound frustrated, but there is clearly something I'm missing here.

Ezra looks to Roman.

"Does she know?"

"I thought it might be too much, but…"

"Know what?" I demand, losing patience.

Ezra's eyes are trained on Roman, who nods as if to give permission to bring me up to speed with whatever the hell is going on.

"Cressida," he begins, "do you remember the photograph I put in your pack?"

"Of course," I say, as I retrieve it from within my suit, all the while wishing that I too had known a time where my grandparents, my mother and Ezra were all together.

"Well," Ezra continues, "did you ever question who took it?"

I hadn't, until now.

Then, making his way from the door, Roman removes a wallet from within his jacket, from which he hands me another photograph. I sit, comparing the two. It captures the same moment – no question: my grandparents and mother stand in the exact same spots, but now Ezra is no longer present. Instead, he has been replaced by another figure, upright, smiling…familiar grey eyes looking into mine through the decades.

"You?"

There is a tear lingering on Roman's cheek as my bewildered stare begins to process what I'm seeing. Back to the photograph, and Roman's arm is around my mother who, this time around, looks more content than I've ever seen her. My eyes scan down slowly, taking in their eyes, their smile, their bodies pulled close to one another, until I finally stop at the sight of their hands – my mother's cradling Roman's, which rests tenderly on her stomach.

I'm trembling. My eyes search frantically for answers, first to Ezra, then to Roman. I feel like the floor has disappeared beneath me.

"It was the hardest thing I've ever done," Roman says, answering an unspoken question. "Our people needed someone to go deep undercover, and no one was more capable than me."

"But." I gasp. "They told me…"

"You have to understand that we wanted nothing more than to tell you, but it was for your own safety. Believe me, we've had people captured, imprisoned, interrogated, even tortured for information. We couldn't risk that happening to you. Then, when I spoke to you upstairs, I knew…I knew you finally understood. Your mother told me about the young woman you were becoming…she was so proud…and I…"

His attention is taken by some movement over my shoulder. My mother stirs, inhaling long and deep which seems to send a wave of relief through the full length of her body. As quickly as it rises, her body slumps back into the sheeting below, however her face twitches into life as if being

160

woken from a deathly sleep, and for the first time in days, her eyes manage to peer through their heavy lids. Her irises wander, struggling for focus, before resting upon me and my heart leaps as I see the pupils flare almost imperceptibly.

"Cres…"

I feel a broad smile break across my face.

"Shhhh, yes, it's me. You're going to be fine now…just rest."

Her head lolls to one side, neck clearly lacking the strength to keep her upright, but the movement takes her eyeline directly towards Roman.

She gasps. Barely audible, but unmistakeable.

I shuffle closer to cradle her head but, as I do, I find her hand on mine. Slowly, she invites Roman to take the other, and before I know what is happening, all three of our hands are together for the first time.

Ever.

Mine, my mother's…and my father's.

A tear escapes the corner of her eye – one of sheer joy.

But it's short-lived…

"So…it's you."

Summerhythe is standing in the doorway, gun drawn.

"Now everything's starting to make sense. Don't move."

Her voice is ice-cold as she activates the comms unit on her lapel.

"This is Summerhythe to Control requesting backup at holding cell 12. 'Brutus' has been found. Repeat – 'Brutus' has been found."

Chapter Thirty-Three

"It doesn't need to be this way, Summerhythe."

Roman speaks with caution, gun still firmly trained upon us, Summerhythe unflinching.

"I know what you saw at The Ether – you know what The Panaceum is capable of – but this is our chance to put right the wrongs of the past. A new world…where all those who helped establish The Panaceum can thrive in it once again."

Four walls. Ceiling. Floor. One exit.

There's no easy escape – that much is clear – and besides attempting to break apart the bed, no weapons to hand. Appealing to Summerhythe's good nature seems as good a plan as any, but it's clear she's not for turning.

"You know, I'd never have guessed it was you. Roman: *Brutus* – it's almost too obvious when you think about it. But no: everyone was fooled, right up to the last minute…and you got so close. Shame."

I look to Ezra, imploring him to search for a solution. His eyes dart around the room to no avail but then, as they settle upon me again, I see them flare at the sight of my hands.

The ring.

I think back to the instructions which accompanied it: SHIELD EYES...BREAK GLASS...RUN.

Well, I don't have a better plan.

My mother already has her eyes closed, so no issue there. I look to Roman: Ezra follows my gaze and nods in affirmation and a silent plan is agreed. Roman is still pleading his case for a better future as I rise to my feet.

"Oh, just leave it," I yell, spitting the words with as much contempt as I can muster, "It's obvious she doesn't have her own opinion. She's been brainwashed...fed the same lies as I was for decades...it's all she knows."

Summerhythe twitches, but still has the gun trained on Roman – I need her full attention. The last thing I want is for her to panic and fire in shock: in that event, at least *I* would be prepared.

"You know," I continue, "I saved your life...more than once. Jonah was intent on killing you, and I pleaded for you. You *let me* plead for you! And then...in that medical facility...you *saw* the conditions of those bodies and you stood there and pretended to care! I mean, what kind of a person..."

"I did *not* pretend to care."

Summerhythe's head tilts, and I can see that her attention is now split, although the gun itself has not wavered.

"Of course, you did," I continue, "you're a murderer. You know all too well what fate your subjecting *thousands* of innocent people to, and you're still standing there defending it: feeding everyone lies about some eutopia that doesn't even exist."

I can see her body twitching now and know that I've hit a nerve. I just need to push a little further.

"The only comfort I have is that one day…*you'll* be lying there: Patient 8. Your skin eating itself alive – all the while, knowing that you could have made a difference and chose not to…like a coward! I hope its agony…"

"Shut up!" Summerhythe screams, swivelling at the hip and pointing the gun squarely between my eyes. As she does, I have already slipped the ring from my finger: I close my eyes tightly and hurl it towards the ground. There's an immediate burst of sound, and then my eyelids glow a shocking red. A flash, and a flicker of warmth, before both the light and heat subside. After the initial impact, I realise I can hear cries of aguish. I open my eyes: it's Summerhythe, reeling in pain – blind and disorientated – on the ground. To my right, Roman and Ezra already have my mother on her feet and are heading as quickly as we can towards the corridor.

Outside, rather than head towards the exit, we appear to head deeper into the bowels of the building.

"If we're lucky, these tunnels should take us at least beyond the cathedral walls," Roman says, trying hard to maintain good pace.

In truth though, my mother is almost a dead weight and the going is slow. I can't help myself.

"How long before Summerhythe comes after us?"

"Two to three minutes, at best," Ezra replies, knowing as well as I do that that seems far from enough time to make an escape. Regardless, we plough on through the darkness. There is no light at all now, and we rely on touch and instinct to guide us. It may work in our favour – if we can't see anything, then hopefully Summerhythe can't either, and if there is more than one tunnel, we may just get lucky and avoid detection.

My brief sense of hope vanishes immediately though as, behind us, a siren begins to wail in the distance.

"Full scale alert – Summerhythe must have raised the alarm."

"What do we do?"

"We keep going," Roman insists. "There must be access to the surface not far from here. Run your hands along the walls for any sign of steps or ladders and keep an eye out for even the tiniest source of light."

There's no denying that our pace has slowed; despite his best efforts, Ezra is waning. I frantically run my hands along the rough surface of the tunnel walls, but there's no sign of any means of escape. We seem to be rounding a bend: all the while I can hear Ezra's breath getting heavier...and then, something else...

Footsteps. A single set. Behind us.

I don't want to alert the others, but the urgency has never been greater.

"Keep pushing!"

We continue to round the corner.

"There!" I cry, louder than I'd intended with Summerhythe bearing down on us.

Still, the unmistakable blue hue appears like a desert mirage, and with newfound energy we scramble towards the light. The sight of sky through the opening above me sends a wave of relief, but I know we're not finished yet. Where I stand marks the end of the tunnel: a solid wall studded with individual iron rungs leading up to a portal – the cover for which appears to have been set to one side...

"There's no way Althea has the strength." Roman gasps. "I'll climb – you and Ezra support from below and I'll haul her up."

I nod, but my mind is torn between receiving the instruction and knowing that we can't have much time now.

With Roman in place above, Ezra and I heave my mother's body into an upright position and raise her arms, until he's able to reach for her and lift as we push from below. It takes immense effort, and at this stage Ezra is no help at all. I can hear my mother's body scraping the wall but push with all my might regardless; there's no time to worry about a few lumps and bruises.

"You next, Cressida." Ezra rasps, he seems barely able to stand.

"No, you next, you're going to need my help."

He doesn't even argue as, wheezing, he pulls himself up onto the first rung. I support from below until Roman is able to reach the neck of his coat from above and take over. Without hesitation, I begin my own ascent…

It's then that the air around me explodes. The bullet whizzes past my earlobe and into the wall in front of me. Shards of ancient stone spray my eyes and despite every effort, I flinch, losing grip of the rung I am clinging to and land in a heap of the floor below. Frantically, my hands search in vain for the ladder…

"Don't move!"

Her voice is panicked and breathless, but unmistakeable.

"Don't move…or *I promise you* I will shoot."

I dare to open my eyes and see the starlit sky above me.

So close…

I rise to my feet.

Overhead, I hear the shuffling of bodies: Roman, Ezra, and my mother. Free. So close to safety.

If I'm captured, they won't leave me…and all of our efforts will be in vain.

If I'm captured, I'll be tortured until death, or until I break my silence…and all of our efforts will be in vain.

If I'm captured…

With a mind of absolute clarity, I extend my spine to its full height, place my hand on the first rung of the ladder and begin to climb.

"I'm warning you…"

I hear the words but allow them to deflect off me.

Another rung.

"Cressida…don't make me do this."

And another.

From above, Roman – my father – lowers a quivering hand.

I feel the night air against my face as I hear Summerhythe setting her feet behind me, and sense her taking aim.

Just one more rung…

Before my hand has a chance to grasp my father's, a shadow, swooping through the darkness like an oversized bat, catches the corner of my eye. I turn just in time to see Summerhythe's head snap backwards and blood spray out like a large red rosette to one side of her forehead. She drops like a stone to the ground below, the dead weight of her limbs crashing to the earth, crunching and making me wince.

Dumbstruck, I frantically scour the darkness for any further signs of an ambush – my skin buzzing with sheer adrenaline – until my eyes settle upon a face which slowly emerges into the moonlight and suddenly all of the pieces fall perfectly into place…

"Jonah?"

Chapter Thirty-Four

I can see the expanding pool of blood forming around Summerhythe's skull, and can only assume her heart is still beating, as a healthy flow still pours from the lesion by her temple. Unconscious, yes, but in the silence, she almost sounds as though she is in a heavy sleep, as my hand reaches towards her. I have no intention of helping; I simply retrieve the throwstick by her side. Having caused the damage, its blood-sleeked surface glistens purple in the blue hue of the tunnel, as moonbeams catch the edges of the engravings which adorn it. My fingers trace over a new addition, towards the base of the weapon: a boy in flight, wings outstretched and cradled in his arms, a girl...

"Cress."

It's Jonah, beside me, a relieved grin spread wide across his face. I can't help but return it. I pass the throwstick and, during the transfer, fix him with a gaze that I can only hope conveys my gratitude, appreciation, and – let's face it – a whole host of other emotions that I can't even begin to process right now.

Jonah wipes down the throwstick and returns it to the holster between his shoulder-blades. His attention shifts over my shoulder.

"Cressida!"

It's my father – although I'm still not used to thinking of him as such. He looks down to Summerhythe, then to Jonah – joining together the dots – before gazing deeper into the tunnel, searching for any signs of backup.

"They won't be far behind. We need to move, now...thank you?"

"Jonah," I reply, softly.

"Thank you, Jonah."

Jonah nods courteously and we waste no time in making our way back to the ladder. As we walk, I can't help but ask.

"How did you find us?"

Jonah gives a wry smile. "I said I would, didn't I? And I wasn't going to leave it to chance..."

I throw a puzzled glance as he continues, "What? You didn't think I gave you that necklace just because I liked you...did you? The council need to know where scouts are at all times."

I don't even give him the satisfaction of seeing my cheeks flush as I turn coolly and begin my ascent to the surface.

The night air feels cool and cleanses my skin – I drink it in in thirsty gulps. A few feet away, my mother is sitting upright, supported by Ezra and manages the faintest of smiles. I rush to her, almost desperate – like a kid at the school gates – and wrap my arms around her tightly. She groans but returns the hug with all the strength she can muster. I release my grip.

"Sorry."

"Don't be," she says, tears welling, "Cress, I have so much –"

"Later," I interrupt, "there'll be a time for all of that."

And there would be…but right now – here – we're still in danger. We need refuge. We need to regroup. We need to recuperate.

I look up to The Panacean Council Building – sirens wailing, searchlights beginning to activate frantically in the distance – and know that our task is only half done.

Right now, I have a mother to revive and to *rediscover*: a selfless freedom-fighter at the forefront of an underground movement against an overbearing oppressor; and a father who…

Well…

I actually *have* a father.

The realisation finally hits me, and my eyes begin to sting.

I feel a hand on my shoulder – it's Jonah, by my side…as ever.

"We need to move," he whispers softly, sensing my tearfulness.

Ezra, my mother, and my father are already making their way towards the shadows ahead. I think of my grandfather, and what it will mean to return his daughter to him safely – the relief, the joy – but one thing will still be missing.

My grandmother.

To save her, we'll need to go somewhere no Panacean has been before and returned to tell the tale…yet.

Heaven awaits us…